PUFFIN BOOKS
THINGS IN CORNERS

There is a strange, pulsing blob in the corner of Theo's
elevator. Gideon looks out of his apartment window and
sees an old lady ... *flying*. And who is the insanely laughing
man in the mirror of the vintage car? You'll find out in this
collection of five deliciously horrifying stories ... and, after
reading them, you'll never look at things in corners the
same way again.

'Even when the mystery is 'explained' and the evil driven
away, you're left with a sense of things not quite 'square',
as if inanimate objects are out of control and human feelings
can blight a landscape.'

ALA *Booklist*

'The author of *Playing Beatie Bow*, one of children's
literature's finest time-travel novels, continues to give
fantasized fiction the hard edges of believable realism.'
Bulletin of the Center for Children's Books, Chicago

'Park creates the most "real" children and adults in the most
simple but telling prose – exciting and resonant.'
Agnes Nieuwenhuizen, Melbourne *Age*

By the same author

For Young Readers

The Ship's Cat
The Hole in the Hill
The Sixpenny Island
The Road under the Sea
The Road to Christmas
Uncle Matt's Mountain
Airlift for Grandee
Ring for the Sorcerer
The Runaway Bus
Nuki and the Sea Serpent
The Muddle-Headed Wombat (series)
Roger Bandy
Callie's Castle
The Gigantic Balloon
Come Danger, Come Darkness
The Big Brass Key
When the Wind Changed
James
Playing Beatie Bow
My Sister Sif

Novels

The Harp in the South
Poor Man's Orange
Missus
The Witch's Thorn
A Power of Roses
Dear Hearts and Gentle People
The Frost and the Fire
Serpent's Delight
Swords and Crowns and Rings

Ruth Park

THINGS IN CORNERS

Puffin Books

Puffin Books
Penguin Books Australia Ltd
487 Maroondah Highway, PO Box 257
Ringwood, Victoria, 3134, Australia
Penguin Books Ltd
Harmondsworth, Middlesex, England
Viking Penguin, A Division of Penguin Books USA Inc.
375 Hudson Street, New York, New York 10014, USA
Penguin Books Canada Limited
10 Alcorn Avenue, Toronto, Ontario, Canada M4V 1E4
Penguin Books (N.Z.) Ltd
182–190 Wairau Road, Auckland 10, New Zealand

First published by Penguin Books Australia, 1989
Published in Puffin, 1990
10 9 8 7

Typeset in Sabon by Bookset Pty Ltd, Melbourne
Made and printed in Australia by Australian Print Group, Maryborough, Vic.

National Library of Australia
Cataloguing-in-Publication data:
Park, Ruth.
  Things in corners.

  ISBN 0 14 032713 4.

  I. Title.

A823.3

Contents

THINGS IN CORNERS

ABOUT THE TIME that Theo Dove turned thirteen, he caught mononucleosis, and had to spend several weeks in bed. The holidays were due, so he did not miss much school. This pleased Theo, as he enjoyed school. He was second in class only because he did not care to be first. It was a boring, disagreeable time. After the first two weeks he was not exactly ill, and not exactly well. The fever and aches and wobbliness were bad enough, but worse was the way he felt, as if a damp grey curtain had been dropped between him and the world.

This way of feeling was not Theo's line at all. He was a sharp, stringy person, always on the go, interested in most things, and ready to do something about them. When he was small he had overheard his mother telling someone that he was a fearless little tough. At the time he hadn't been quite sure how to think of himself, and he had been much taken by the description. It had been no sweat living up to it ever since. But after the mono, he didn't much care for anything. Not even – except politely, of course – in the house-moving, that had happened in his fourth week of being sick. Then the Doves left Parramatta, and moved to a brand-new development east of the Nepean River. Macquarie Meads, it was called. It was a giant leap forward for the family because Cheapies, the supermarket people for whom Mr Dove worked, had opened a branch there, and Mr Dove was to be manager.

Feebly Theo lay in bed and listened to his mother being rapturous about Dad moving up the ladder. Flabbily he sat on the lounge wrapped in a blanket while his bed was being carted off to the removalists' van. Totteringly he was helped into the car, and carried away into the sunset to the new unit.

He felt as if someone had slipped his backbone out, but he refused to go to bed.

'No way, Mum,' he said. 'Not on our first day here.'

He sat in a chair near the kitchen door, with a beam laboriously pegged on his face to match the one that flitted like sunshine across his mother's, as she cooked their first dinner. She kept interrupting the process every three minutes by running to the window and blissfully crying: 'I can see the river. Oh, Ted, I can see the lovely hills. I've always wanted hills. And the smell of everything in here, Ted – all new and clean and painty, no spooks at all!'

Ted was Mr Dove. He hugged Theo's mother, whoofling in her neck to make her shiver and squeal. He was excited, even a bit awed, at being a branch manager at last, responsible for making Cheapies' new store really buzz.

The firm's real name was Cheapest Ltd, but of course it was never called that.

Mr Dove was a skinny brown man with a hearing-aid that nearly drove him up the wall with whistles and crackles. Theo loved him fiercely, so was pretty offhand with him. Various things about his father made his heart almost stop with a kind of pity. For instances, the sidewhiskers the old man had sprouted for some unfathomable reason. They were like little grey wings, pinfeathers. Real sad.

Naturally there were plenty of things about his father that set Theo's teeth on edge. Yet it was touching that a grown man – old, in fact – didn't realise that smoking cigarettes in a charred holder the colour of sick could make other persons actually nauseated. And there was the way he held a fork, like a pencil. And the back of his neck, wrinkled exactly like a second forehead. Theo hated himself for finding anything at all about his father that he didn't like. But he was honest, and had to admit these things.

But now, seeing his parents so happy, he was happy too, as if he were a reflection. Whether that were the reason, or the new home was, or whatever, he began to feel steadily better.

It was great to wake up in the morning and not wish he was still asleep. Still, a week or so passed before he was fit enough to go downstairs and look around the place.

The unit was on the fifth floor of a ten-storey building. The developing company had wanted to make all the unit blocks twenty and thirty floors high, but the conservationists and the Down With Progress societies had shrieked, and the company had been forced to make their residential buildings smaller, and further apart, so that the river and its sandy flats, and the Blue Mountains behind, could be seen.

Theo walked slowly down the stairs, legs rickety, a gone sensation in his stomach. However, he reached the bottom and surveyed what was going to be the garden – a wasteland of raw soil, with a circle of trembling infant willows sticking up out of it, and a funny-shaped area of round river stones arranged around two bushes of dry sabre leaves edged in yellow. There was a fan of concrete which spread under the building to become the parking yard.

Theo shivered, not because everything looked so stark, for time would fix that, but because the wind was like a knife. It smelled of burning leaves and a sweetish dampness, and he remembered that he had been indoors more than a month, the year had moved on, and very soon it would be winter. But he couldn't help approving of everything, the serene clouds gliding over the huge sky, the agreeably scungy smell of the Nepean, the fact that he wouldn't have to change schools, but would continue to travel to Parramatta every day.

He felt that he'd be fine to walk up the stairs again, but he had promised his mother he'd go up in the lift. So he stepped into it. It, too, smelled of varnish, and new rubber flooring, and had golden lattice doors in an Oriental pattern, rather classy. He punched the button, and the lift moaned upwards.

It was then that Theo noticed he was not alone in the lift. There was something crouched in the back corner against the wall. For the first three seconds Theo thought it was some weird bundle of yuk that someone had left there. Then he saw it pulsing slowly, like a sea anemone, and he realised it was alive.

He was stunned. There was no other word for it. He couldn't even move away from it, just stood there, freezing, staring. It was about the size of a medium dog, formless, as if it were made of three-quarters-set jelly. It looked rather like jelly, too, with a faint sheen, almost but not quite translucent, like a slug. It was pearly grey, with darker, wet-looking areas.

The bottom of it spread out, as if it had melted a little, and near where its chest might have been were two half-formed blobs like hands or paws. It was rounded on top, as if for a head, but this bit was turned away towards the corner.

It gave off an unmistakable feeling of affliction and helplessness. A long shudder passed over it, and two semi-circular bulges on the front of what Theo thought was its head began to quiver, like eyelids about to open.

Involuntarily Theo's mouth opened to let loose the kind of yell only heard in monster films, but all that came out was a croak. At that moment the lift stopped, the door wheezed open, and Theo stumbled out into the passage.

The world turned spangly black. Dimly he heard the lift moaning downwards, his mother speaking to him. He managed to walk, leaning on her, his eyes still shut because he was afraid to open them. He found himself on the living-room lounge, a cold wind blowing in from the balcony, a smell of cooking, everything normal. His mother clucked around.

'Too much for you. Shouldn't have let you go downstairs. Are you all right, darling? I wonder if I should call the doctor?'

Theo managed to say, 'No, Mum. Silly. Okay now. Sorry,' and jerk himself upright. It was true that his body was beginning to feel all right, but his mind was going round and round, yelling desperately that he couldn't have seen that thing in the corner of the lift. He must have imagined it.

At the memory of its shapelessness, the pulpy look of its flesh, he almost chucked. He even made a throw-up noise, and his mother dived for a basin. But nothing happened. He lay back, shaking and cold.

'You overdid it, poor old kid,' said his mother, and he let it go at that. By the time his father came home, and was told, and sympathised with Theo, it seemed too late to say anything. Anyway, Theo doubted whether he could have said anything, even in his worst moments of horror after lurching out of the lift. Looking back on it, the thing, its weirdness, his shameful terror – it all seemed like a bad dream. But he knew perfectly well it wasn't. It was so real he was afraid to close his eyes in case he saw it again, imprinted on the inside of his eyelids.

Underneath his amazement and consternation there was a question, rising inexorably, no matter how he tried to suppress it. 'Why was it so sad?'

In bed, he tried closing his eyes, and saw the usual green spectre of the light bulb's filaments, and nothing else. The thing lived in the lift then, and not inside his head. Exhausted, he fell asleep and had his usual dreams, visual babblings, with a scene or two out of his dream serial, which was based on his life after he was sent to Hilltop Homes for Children, where Mum and Dad had found him and, as they'd told him countless times, exclaimed 'That's the boy for us!'

Theo had vaguely thought it queer that he couldn't remember a single thing about his pre-Hilltop life, even though he'd been over four when his real mother put him up for adoption. You'd think, pondered Theo, that a four-year-old kid would remember *something* – being smacked, or taken to the zoo or the dentist, or leaving his mother for the last time or something important like that. In earlier years he had tried to remember his mother's face, her dress, her voice or anything at all. But nothing seemed to be there. She didn't appear even in his dreams. When he was younger and more outspoken about his private feelings, he had sometimes asked Mum about her. 'All we know is that she loved you dearly,' said Mum. 'Look at the name she gave you. Theodore means given by God.'

Actually Theo couldn't stick either end of his name. Theo was pretty awful, and Dove was the kind of name that caused other people to make dumb jokes, like calling him Lovey Dovey. The name, though, had served a good purpose. It had made him unwilling to stand any kind of teasing or shoving around. Before he was eight, he had been in so many fights that one teacher warned the other kids, 'This Dove pecks.' Theo had been proud of that, and still was.

When young, he had always liked hearing what Mum said, that his real mother thought he was a gift of God, and not a pain in the arse. It had been like sunshine, warming him through and through. Of course, as he got older, the whole thing made him feel scratchy, and he stopped asking Mum to tell him about his real mother.

'She was young, and she was sick, and she called you Theodore, so she must have loved you.'

That was all he knew about where he came from, and the first two bits might have been cooked up by the Sisters who ran Hilltop, anyway. The only thing of which he was sure, and the only thing that mattered was that the Doves were his real unshakeable Mum and Dad, and he'd die if things were otherwise. In the midst of wondering just how he'd die – heart failure, wasting away, or what – he fell asleep, and when he awakened in the morning he felt stronger, hungrier, the grey curtain between him and the world almost gone. That was his outside. On his inside he had this dreary knowledge, that he had seen something shockingly real and scary in the lift, and he didn't know why.

Many times he almost blurted the story out to his father. He knew that Dad wouldn't think he was lying, or anything like that. But somehow he could not get the first words out. It all sounded so mad that he was embarrassed. Still, he thought about it, what the thing was, what it meant, if anything; why a ghost, if that's what it was, should haunt a brand-new building in a brand-new suburb.

Then he thought that perhaps there'd been a house there before, and there'd been some ghastly murder in it. He knew there'd been coaching inns along the old Castlereagh Road, near which Macquarie Meads had been planned. Okay then, suppose there was an inn, and there'd been the murder of an unsuspecting traveller. Theo could see him in his mind's eye – tall, with a blue beaver hat. Oily kind of Mine Host in long apron, horses jingling, stableboy with sly, squinty eyes leading them away, welcome, welcome, good sir. Traveller drugged – wine, helpless on bed, in comes sinister Mine Host with glittering chopper. Well, that was enough to cause a place to be haunted, but why by a spongy grey thing, and why in a lift?

Theo knew that the crunch would come when he travelled in the lift again. But no matter how he lashed himself with accusations of cowardice, his flesh crept when he thought of that lift. He'd get to the door, turn away as if he'd remembered something (this was to fool other people waiting) and clatter away down the stairs. For by now he was back at school, though not allowed to do any football training as yet.

Just the same he was filled with a deep, voiceless shame. It was his terror he didn't want to let his parents know about. He might have been a fearless little tough in his young days, but now he felt about as tough as a boiled egg. He fiercely resolved that he'd do something about this, try the lift again, perhaps when someone was in it. School was no problem. The college did have a lift, but it was reserved for the more senile teachers. The young ones belted up the stairs with the boys, and the middle-aged ones marched up briskly, saying it was good for their hearts, but looking slightly mauve at the top.

Theo was busy one way and another, and sometimes he almost forgot the thing. Mum worked mornings in a children's creche not far away, and Dad slaved away at Cheapies early and late. The shopping centre was arranged around a square – it would be the village square when the grass grew – and was intended to have a colonial look. There were even some tiny shops with shingled eaves and bottle-glass windows, Harriet's Kitchen and Abigail's Pots, and so on. Even Cheapies had a dark timber facade, with a trellis up which an ornamental grapevine swung hand over hand. It was inside that the supermarket was cheap – bare floors, trolleys that squealed, shelves stocked with brands no one had ever heard of, a single angry girl at the checkout.

Dad worked like a dog, mostly in shirt sleeves, everywhere at once, shoving trains of trolleys out of the way, standing in the loading dock, clipboard in hand, always hovering over the stock, pushing that packet forward, that tin back, making endless notes. Theo watched his father silently, knowing that Dad had been born with a plastic spoon in his mouth. Funny how some people had the knack of making everything go easily for themselves. Others just naturally did everything the hard way.

Mum was a maintenance corps for Dad. She kept him well, soothed, cheered, his shoes shimmering, his clothes pressed, replaced at intervals. Theo wondered whether Cheapies knew they were really getting two people for one man's wage. He thought they probably did.

In a way they were even getting Theo part time. Often

on Sundays he went up and helped Dad check stock. And he was in charge of keeping the car looking as smart as an eight-year-old Datsun could look. Passionately Theo wanted Dad to have a smart car. Nothing fabulous like a Mercedes, but something image-making. The Datsun passed on the image of a decent old dad with a hearing-aid. Not a branch manager. Not even a branch manager in a new suburb faked-up by developers in a part of Sydney where no one in previous history had ever wanted to live.

But still, some day when the trees grew and there were more people, Macquarie Meads would be all right. For a good part of the time Theo was absolutely contented.

Then, one Sunday morning, when he and his father were at the shop checking over a truckload of canned food that had been delivered the previous afternoon, Theo absentmindedly blew it.

There was a storage basement under Cheapies, and a huge goods lift to shift the stuff down or up. The storeman had loaded the platform of the lift with cases of tins before he clocked out the previous day, so Theo's father said: 'Take that down, will you, son, and start pulling them out? I'll be down to help stack directly.'

Theo jumped into the lift, clanged the doors to, and was on his way before he thought twice. Suddenly he did. In the same instant he saw from the corner of his eye something pulpy and grey to his right. The lift hit bottom with the cushiony bounce it always gave and Theo crashed against the door, clawing at the lever, shouting. As he leaped away from It, he had seen that a pile of tins and It both occupied the same corner. Through the glutinous flesh, he read the words 'Peeled Tomatoes'.

As the door opened, he staggered out, hit the corner of a crate and subsided. When he came to, his father was kneeling beside him, tapping his face, saying, 'Theo, mate, what's up?'

'Sorry Dad,' he mumbled. 'Couldn't help it. The lift.'

'The lift, what's the matter with the lift?'

Theo almost told him. The words were in his mouth. He looked at his father, saw he was an old, anxious, overworked man, and shut it again. He just couldn't. He couldn't add to Dad's problems.

But his father's forehead smoothed out, he looked as if some good thought had struck him, and he blurted! 'You mean, when you're in a lift, you feel all shut in?'

'Do I ever,' said Theo, in heartfelt tones.

'Was that the matter before, when you came over queer, back home?'

Theo nodded. And so off he went on a path of half-truth that was more difficult to put right than not talking at all.

It took a long time before he would agree to go to the doctor.

He kept moaning, 'Don't bug me, Mum. I'm all right. Aw gee, Mum, get off my back, won't you?'

Sometimes he made her laugh. Sometimes she made him laugh. He knew that Dad, as well, wanted him to be sounded out by a doctor. But the old man never said so.

'What's so important about lifts?' Theo asked his mother querulously.

'It's not just the lift,' explained his mother. 'That might happen to anyone. I mean, all kinds of things come over people. Like having a craze for peanuts, or hating to wear blue. I just want to know why this happened just now, whether your health isn't a hundred per cent. You were pretty sick with that rotten glandular fever.'

Theo had to agree. The remembrance of his illness cheered him. That might be the reason for this freaky business. There was something out of order, his eyes perhaps. He became quite lively, and after school one day went off to the doctor.

The doctor had already treated him for the mononucleosis, so they were old acquaintances. He was a little flat oval man like a tick, with a good-humoured expression. Mrs Dove had already rung and briefed him, for he said pleasantly, 'Been having a brush with claustrophobia, have we?'

Theo nodded.

'Not to worry. You've had a bad virus infection and that kind of thing often leaves little nervous upsets behind it.'

While he examined Theo, he rattled off a few dull yarns about other people's phobias. Theo waited hopefully, longing to hear that there was something amiss, but naturally not potentially fatal. The doctor jotted down this and that, and Theo returned to earth to hear him saying '. . . kept all her wardrobe doors open in case she was accidentally locked into one.'

'Oh, I don't mind wardrobes and stuff,' said Theo. 'It's just lifts.'

The doctor rolled up his black blood-pressure gadget and said thoughtfully, 'Could you, for instance, go and stand in my long cupboard over there?'

'Sure,' said Theo, and he went over and got into the cupboard, which mostly held golf clubs and old raincoats. While he was in there he realised he had been dumb. No one was going to believe that claustrophobia applied only to lifts.

He thought then that he'd break down and tell the doctor that lifts now had a grey thing in the corner and he couldn't bear it. But he couldn't. To his horror he felt his throat stiffen, his nose block up, his eyes burn. He tried to get up and go out, but the tears were too fast. He was reduced to putting down his head and trying to hide in his handkerchief.

The doctor was kind and matter of fact. He gave Theo a prescription, just a mild tonic, he said. 'Physically,' he said, 'you're a perfect specimen. That eye doesn't bother you nowadays, does it? Just slides a bit when you're tired? That's nothing. Tell your mother to give me a ring when she has time, will you?'

Theo took the tonic, and resolved, over and over again, that he would beat the thing. No imaginary gluggy blob, born of germs and fever, was going to lick him. But it took a mighty effort before he was able to carry out his plan.

Twice each week, Wednesdays and Fridays, he tried himself out on the lift. He went down to the third floor, where people hardly ever bothered to use it, and he knew he would find it empty. Empty of humans, that is.

Every Tuesday and Thursday night he kept waking up in a cold sweat because of the day it would be tomorrow. Every Wednesday and Friday morning he couldn't wait to do his trial run and get it over with. The way he did it and not blow his mind altogether with fright was to step into the lift and allow the door nearly to close. He took a ballpoint pen with him, and held it against the door as it was sliding to. Until the door was about a centimetre off the side, the lift was empty of all but himself, glaring bright and empty. Then all at once, the thing was there, crouched in its corner, it gelatinous skin gleaming moistly.

Almost in the same instant Theo's finger punched the OPEN DOOR button upon which it had been resting, and he leaped out into the passage, heart thundering, breath stuck for a moment before he could get it going again. Sometimes the lift stayed there, bright and empty. Other times the door softly closed at once and whined away, leaving Theo panting, hopeless.

He could have whimpered with despair.

Other times he thought things could have been worse. A person could certainly go throughout life without lifts. It might have been that the thing haunted the corners of loos, and then where would he have been? Perhaps the best thing would be to wipe lifts out of his life and just pretend the whole thing hadn't happened. That's what many people would do.

But Theo couldn't. He wasn't many people, only himself. After all, the thing made no threatening gestures. It did not even look at him. It might be different if it had come and sat on his chest and chewed his neck in the middle of the night.

Big deal. He still hated and feared it. The strain of Wednesdays and Fridays was almost too much for him. He slipped to fourth in class. That happened after finding the old woman in the lift. He saw her there, winter coat with furry collar, fluffy hat, and decided to take his chances. The door shut. The old lady said, 'Chilly, eh dear?' and they were on their way down before Theo saw that his fellow passenger was standing right on It, her solid shoe surrounded by a thick grey gauze, and the hem of her coat half-seen through its head, where the hidden eyeball twitched as if any moment now the lid would rise.

Theo was nearly sick that time. He had to go into the parking area to lean against a wall, ears booming.

His appetite had gone, and he found it hard to get to sleep. When he did, he seemed only a few centimetres below the surface, a half-taught swimmer, choking, struggling, emerging for a breath and sinking again. There were dreams in glorious technicolour, or rather, scraps of dreams, like a book dropping open, to show him a picture or half a page and then snapping shut again. Most of these dreams related to Hilltop, like getting marooned on a forbidden ladder, and Sister Clement, a nice old lady made of black wool, coming along and picking him off and giving him a pink musk lolly. And playing the triangle in the band at Christmas. The Home doctor fitting his first spectacles and explaining about lazy eyes and teaching him exercises to make his come out of its corner.

Quite reasonable things to remember, thought Theo, puzzling why they had come back just now and in such gaudy colour. He often caught his mother looking at him anxiously. Then one day his father told him he had received from the doctor a referral to a psychiatrist. Theo could scarcely believe his ears.

'You think I've gone bonkers!'

'Ah, no, of course I don't, mate. It's just that the doc thinks that sometime something frightening must have happened to you in a lift.'

'It never did!'

'But perhaps you don't remember it. Perhaps it was before you went to the Home, Theo. That's what psychiatrists are for, to help you remember.'

Theo was outraged. So was his mother. She was an old-fashioned woman who thought of psychiatrists only as doctors who treated insane people. Theo's father explained that psychiatrists were often able to help the unhappy or confused.

'I'm not unhappy or confused!'

'All right, all right,' said Mr Dove. 'A personality problem, then.'

His wife looked as if someone had dropped a stone on her. She said in a low voice, 'You mean because he's adopted, don't you, Ted?'

Mrs Dove had a rather loud, merry voice. It was one of the things Theo most enjoyed about her. This low, whispery voice made his skin positively creep. He must have looked frightened, for his father said. 'Needless to say, I wouldn't pressure you to keep the appointment, mate. But I'll be frank. I do want you to go. I want you to be yourself again in every way.'

It was hard for Theo to say no to his father. Too hard. But what really sent him to the psychiatrist was his mother's hardcore belief that the man was the joke figure of popular myth. He felt he had to disprove this, otherwise she'd always be sore, believing that Dad had sent his only son off to a shrink because he thought he'd flipped. When he agreed to keep the appointment, Mrs Dove courageously said she'd go with him. Poor Dad was so busy and had too many worries already.

They went to Sydney, to Macquarie Street, where most specialists had their consulting rooms. They walked up the stairs, eight flights, to Dr Amby's office.

Theo had little idea what to expect. To his vexation he began to feel a rising alarm. When he saw how frightened his mother was, the alarm turned into anger. At her, for being scared. At himself, for agreeing to something that was spooking him before it even happened.

The waiting room had a self-consciously non-clinical look — flowers and pictures, and a wood fire burning, and a cat muffed down in front of the fire. Theo locked his gaze on this cat, because he didn't want to see his mother's fingers clenched about her handbag like bars of iron.

A patient came out of the consulting room, and Theo flicked him a hard look to see if you could tell. But he was just a man, chunky and sunburned like a golf pro.

'Nice old puss,' he said, tickling the muffed-up cat.

Mrs Dove smiled a clenched smile. Then it was Theo's turn. The receptionist wouldn't allow Mrs Dove to go in with Theo, as she wanted to. 'Later, perhaps if he,' she gestured at the door, 'needs to see you.'

Mrs Dove sank back, trembling. As he was led away, Theo could see her vibrating faintly. He gave her an encouraging grin. He was feeling hopeful again. He had made up his mind that he would tell this Dr Amby everything. No need to feel shy, as if the doctor would fall off his chair in a fit when he heard. He probably had patients who kept lions and tigers in their heads.

Almost eagerly he went into the consulting room. He had formed a picture of Dr Amby, someone grave and wise, a TV shrink in a white jacket. A quirky little smile.

But the psychiatrist was young and trendy, wearing a short-sleeved blue shirt and faded jeans with thready seams.

'Hi,' he said.

Like lightning Theo took a dislike to him, his stuck-on face, his hair, curly and ginger, his voice. Especially his knees, which pressed against the jeans like two little oval lids.

Theo had never cared for adult knees, but these were away out on their own. He certainly wasn't going to break down and blab that he saw things in lifts to anyone with knees like those. Theo knew that he had steadfast eyes; he now turned these steadfast eyes on Dr Amby, and answered his questions forbiddingly. They were back to old claustrophobia at once and Theo treated that with truthful monosyllables. He wasn't really certain that Knees didn't know all along that, while he was getting truth, he wasn't getting the whole truth. There might have been just a glimpse of patient disappointment on his face. Because of this, and because Theo knew very well he was not giving the guy a fair go, he tried to dislike him even more. He found it easy to despise him because he was so snide. He must have been over thirty, yet here he was wearing jeans instead of an oldies' three-piece suit.

So he kept looking at him steadfastly, and pretty soon Dr Amby groped around for a prescription pad.

'That'll do for now, Theo. Don't want to bore you. I'll just give you a few soothies to ease you along until next week.'

He had to go back three times before his parents gave up. Theo knew he was being dumb. This Amby might have been able to help, that was what he was there for. It was no use expecting him to guess that Theo saw things in lifts, because that perhaps wasn't at all a common thing. But even if Theo had wanted to talk, he wouldn't have been able to. At least, not without a lot of yelling and blubbering. Which wasn't his scene at all.

But the guy was trying, truly trying, so as a sort of bonus Theo told him about the dream he'd had for years of someone crying. Dr Amby's eyes didn't exactly light up, but anyone could see he was pleased.

'Ah, you're adopted, aren't you?'

'Yes, but –'

Theo wanted to tell him he was wrong, it wasn't a little kid crying, he was off the track. But Dr Amby enthusiastically plunged into a long series of questions about how he got on with Mum and Dad, and did he ever think of his real mother, and so on, so Theo gave up, just answering truthfully and looking steadfast.

'We'll get it by the tail eventually,' said Dr Amby. He was kind, a right person, in spite of his knees. He was also lavish with the pills. Altogether Theo had blue zonkers, and pinkish ones, and capsules red at one end and black at the other. He had taken only three or four of the lot, flushing the others down the loo.

'I can't imagine why you're not feeling better, darling,' said his mother, as though all those wasted dollars had been honour-bound to work a vast change in him.

He tried again to explain. 'Mum, there's nothing the matter. I just feel choked in lifts. It'll wear off. And I'm not going back to that Amby again, it's just a waste of time and money.'

His father argued, his mother got tearful. But eventually they agreed to leave him alone. There was no more of that casting of worried looks at him, as though Mum expected to catch him talking excitedly to himself, or poking forks up his nose. He thought that maybe this was because Mum had concluded that the psychiatrist hadn't found that being adopted had thrown him crooked in some way.

Yet, was this true? He had heard that adopted children often had problems of one kind or another. Still, he had never noticed that he had any. His satisfaction with his parents was probably part sloppy gratitude for their choosing him, a rowdy six-year-old with glasses and a cast in one eye. He realised that. But it was also because they were terrific people and he liked them. Certainly he'd sometimes had a curiosity about his mother, what was her name, why she hadn't wanted to keep him, and so on. But most of the questions he asked were just childish gabble. He accepted what his parents had told him.

Still, Theo couldn't imagine why any woman would give away her kid like something valueless. Even worse to give away a kid old enough to know people, be scared and lonely.

'Gift of God,' thought Theo, and a huge sneer filled his soul. He couldn't imagine Mum giving him away, ever. She'd fight like a wildcat.

Theo was proud of that. Being adopted was not at the bottom of his fear. But the fear was there, and Theo knew that if he ever was to get rid of it, he would have to front up to the thing, even if it opened its eyes. The very idea made him nauseated. Inside he was yelling, 'I can't, I can't!'

He went down to seventh in class. He was dropped from the football team because he had slowed up so. He still woke up a lot at night, and he had stopped having technicolour dreams about Hilltop. Almost every night now he had his crying dream, which was in black and white, with someone sobbing and sobbing, and terrible feelings of sadness. Doggedly he went on practising in the lift, being sick and giddy before and after, but not giving up.

It had become a matter of life and death to him. One day he would close the lift door, and the thing would not be there. Alternatively, one day it would be there, but he would have the courage to look at it, stare it out, all the way to the bottom.

And this day did come. Afterwards he thought that the happening was because of sheer desperation, because he felt that the Theo Dove he had once been was leaking away out of a corner somewhere, and that pretty soon he'd be one of those weakies that everyone pushed around.

This realisation made him so furious that he could scarcely stand it. He did his homework, still furious. Mum was bashing about in the kitchen, so he called out, 'Going for a walk, Mum,' and went straight out to the lift.

He pressed the button. His heart began to bump, skip. His skin got cold and knobbly. He kept thinking, 'Now or never, now or never,' and the lift slid up in front of him, and the door opened.

Even then he knew he could escape if he wished, but he didn't. He jumped in so fast he almost hit the back wall, and by the time he'd turned around, the door had closed, the lift had begun to move downwards, and the thing was squatting in the corner.

He kept his eyes shut, leaning against the opposite corner, dripping with sweat. Then, without moving his head, he shot it a glance – grey, jellified, its bump of a head bowed, half-turned away. He croaked, 'What do you want?' and was instantly terrified in case it answered. He hadn't thought of its voice. Soggy and blurred, it would be, coming from a shapeless shape like that. The feeling of sadness suddenly was overpowering. It filled the lift, it vibrated inside Theo's head, and he knew it was the same hopeless, helpless sadness that filled the crying dream.

As if the thing had read his thoughts, its head sluggishly turned, its eyelids quivered, and it opened its eyes and looked at him.

They were beautiful, sorrowful brown eyes. Eyes he knew.

He let out a loud cry, the lift bounced on the ground floor, the thing became completely transparent, wavered, and vanished. The door slid aside, and there was his father, face pale, staring at him aghast.

'Theo! Was that you shouting? What is it, what's the matter?'

Dad didn't take him upstairs, or fetch a doctor. He just led him under the building to where the old car was parked, and they sat inside with the windows up. Theo talked and talked, sometimes laughing, sometimes crying, while Mr Dove twiddled his hearing-aid agitatedly, sometimes hearing Theo all right, and often not, and occasionally getting a whistle that made him jump.

Theo told Dad about his crying dream – how it wasn't a child crying but a woman, a young woman with brown eyes.

'She didn't call me Theo, Dad, she called me Tay-O, that's what she called me, Dad.'

And about the squeezes and hugs, and the chases around the floor, and being taken out in new blue shorts, only a dog bowled him over and the pants got muddy and he yelled and got hugged again. And ice cream, both of them eating ice creams. Laughter, and crawling into her bed and holding tight to her long black plait of hair as he went to sleep.

And then being taken to Hilltop, and missing her, and not eating, and always looking through the gate, and finally realising without being told that he would never see her again.

'That's when I must have made up my mind that I'd forget,' he marvelled, 'and I did. But the memories were there all the time.' Now that he had started to talk, he could scarcely stop. He told it all over again to Mum, who listened with tears in her eyes.

'Poor girl, poor girl,' she murmured. 'How terrible to have to give you up. How brave.'

Without a complaint, Theo went with Dad to see Dr Amby, to find out what he made of it all. This time Dr Amby was wearing a white doctor's jacket, and Theo liked him much more.

Dad said, 'You won't want me in there,' but Theo made him go into the consulting room, because Dad was part of anything, good or bad, that happened to him. He retold the story to Dr Amby, remembering even more things this time, the awful, poisonous, little-kid anger that had filled him, when at last he knew that his mother would not come back. Telling about it didn't upset him any more. The bawling and laughing and ceaseless talking in the front seat of the old car had washed him clean.

'Tay-O,' said Dad. 'So she was a foreign girl, Italian or Greek maybe. The sisters said she became sick, poor girl. So that's where you got your brown eyes, mate.'

Dr Amby explained it to them both, how Theo had repressed all these memories because of his loneliness and anger at his mother, and how they'd just kept quiet until he was weakened and sensitised by the mononeucleosis. Then they took shape, an ugly shape, because his feelings were ugly. He was afraid to look at the thing because deep down in his mind he knew that it would bring back memories which he thought were cruel and hurtful.

'I think that as your health improved, the hallucination would have vanished anyway, but it's so much better that you faced it and recognised it. Now you understand that what you thought were disturbing memories aren't so at all.'

Theo and his father rode down in the lift. It was just a lift smelling faintly of antiseptic, as the psychiatrist's office had done. Probably his cat did, too.

Theo's head was full of half-remembered words and happenings. He felt sure there were a thousand things he was going to remember about the years before he went to Hilltop, and they were all good. That girl, his real mother – he had been happy with her, and she with him.

His brown eyes might have come from her; possibly he was Italian or Greek, and that was interesting, but the thing to be sure of was that he wasn't really made up of bits and pieces of other people. He was Theo Dove, and there had never been anyone exactly like him, and never would be again. Mum was Mum, and Dad was Dad, and that was that.

He and Dad walked out into Macquarie Street, and it was a very bright day.

WHERE FREEDOM IS

THE FIRST WEEK of the winter holidays Gideon had spent with his classmate Birrell Hobby on the Hobby property near the Queensland border. He had had a wonderful and alarming time, and was still thinking over parts of it. He also had an uneasy sensation that the Hobbys had found him one big drag.

'You must come again, Donk,' Birrell had said, as he saw Gideon off at the railway station, but Gideon was certain he would never get another invitation. This knowledge, that he had been tried and found wanting, and yet did not know why, angered him all the way down to Sydney. By the time he unkinked his legs and jumped down to the platform to be welcomed by his sister Ludie's husband, Valentine, he felt as surly as he had ever been in his life.

He had met Valentine only once before, and the man hadn't improved in the meantime. To start with, his name was pronounced Valenteen. Gideon could just see those two e's peering out like Valentine's kind, mushy little eyes. Seeing that Valentine's surname was Pozzi, you'd expect those eyes to be a decent colour, black or brown. But instead they were a flowery blue.

Valentine had never grown out of the great hairy era and so his whole top end looked as if something had burst — a seed pod, or cotton boll. He had feeble fair hair, and to have feeble fair hair seemed to Gideon to be an offence against heaven and earth. With cruel scorn he looked at the hair already giving up the ghost on the somewhat bumpy top of Valentine's head. At twenty-eight he'd have a hole there.

It was completely beyond Gideon how Ludie could bear having this person around. Cuddling up to him must be like nestling with a spider. And the way his surname was pronounced – Potsy, like some vile Ocker nickname. Ludie Potsy. He hated it. He burned with embarrassment for his sister. Heaven knew that Louise Bray wasn't all that classy but it was better than Ludie Potsy.

'But I really love it,' laughed Ludie, when he ventured to remark on this come-down. 'Everyone smiles when they hear it. It's great!'

Ludie was nineteen. She was a hairdresser and a greenie and a vegetarian. Valentine was something at Sydney University, a research fellow or tutor. They lived on the thirtieth floor of a block of units in Neutral Bay. It was called Cassia Court. The block of units stuck straight up in the air like a ruler; the unit itself was like a prison cell with chipboard built-ins. It was on a corner of the building. The wind wasped around it from all directions, and when the curtains hadn't been drawn, sky, sea, the tops of other unit blocks, the arch of the Harbour Bridge and such rushed in through the windows with almost horrifying vitality. Everywhere Gideon looked there was something, mostly making a hideous row.

He longed for the groves of trees around the college in Bowral, curdy greens in spring and summer and all kinds of elegant ghost shapes in winter. Or the fabulous tame jungle around the Hobbys' homestead; bougainvillea twisted in the tree tops, and wild orchids, and smells of damp decay, half-sweet, half-piggish.

One thing about Ludie's unit, though, he was able to have a bedroom to himself. If you could call it a bedroom. It was about twice as big as a loo. But Ludie had painted it a sharp yellow that neutralised most of the blue that barged in, and from the window there was a bizarre view of soaring walls, and flat parapeted roofs bristling with TV aerials. With faint pleasure Gideon realised that he might be able to have a bit of fun with his binoculars, a good pair that had been his mother's last gift to him before she left for England.

Valentine rat-scratched on the door.

'Ludie won't be long. I rather fancy myself as a chef, so I hope you're hungry. Have a shower if you'd like to.'

It was only a few minutes before Ludie clopped in. She wore Dr Scholl health sandals with wooden soles and a dolphin smile painted on their fronts. There was a ring of city dirt on the hem of her long purplish dress. She kicked off the shoes and gave Gideon a frantic hug. He made his body as much like a plank as possible, but inside he had a fearful melting feeling as if he were going to bawl, or perhaps chuck. He pulled away before either of these disasters could happen, and made a pass at Ludie's frail jaw with his fist.

'Oh, Gid! To think I've got you for two whole weeks!'

She didn't wait for a reply, but whipped off her jacket and showed her chickeny little shoulder blades. She made a flying leap at Valentine, and buried her nose with every appearance of joy in his whiskers. Twitching with disgust, Gideon went off and had his shower. Dinner was a trial of strength, too. Valentine had made an omelette like a sick sea thing, withered and helpless, sprinkled with herbs of offensive flavour.

'If this is gourmet cooking,' thought Gideon, 'I'll stick to peanut butter sandwiches.'

The fortnight before he could return to school stretched before him like a desert. In bed that night he was seized with real panic as he thought of the long summer holidays coming up at Christmas. Would he have to spend it here with Valentine and dying omelettes?

Before his mother's remarriage he and Mum, and often Ludie, had gone away together, even if it were only to some crummy beach cottage. But still, it was a holiday, picnics and talks and family rubbish and stuff. It probably hadn't entered Mum's head, when she married that old man, that there'd be nowhere for him to go for his holidays. Gideon groaned, punched his pillow, wished it could have been Birrell Hobby's head, went to sleep feeling sick and sour.

It was a relief that Ludie was out working all day, and for most of every day Valentine was not there, either. The two of them were concerned about this; they apparently thought he was pining for their company. He managed to convince them that there was enough in Sydney for him to go to, and look at, and explore, to keep him busy for a month.

Ludie said, 'Just as long as you aren't hanging around here fretting.'

'Fretting about what?' he asked.

Ludie frowned. 'Don't you play games with me, Gideon Bray. I know how mad you were when Mum decided to marry Dr Aarons.'

'You're joking,' said Gideon.

'Don't you want to talk about it?' persisted Ludie. 'Oh, do, Gid. It always helps.'

But Gideon wouldn't, and Ludie had to scamper off to catch her bus, swearing because she was late.

In fact, Gideon did spend most of his time in the unit. He felt tired and half-poisoned, possibly by Valentine's gourmet food.

Once he took a bus out to Avalon to look at his old

home – their old home where he and Ludie had lived all those years ago with their mother and father, and life had been secure and unchangeable. The new people had taken off the faded striped window canopies that Dad had had such trouble to put up; he had been a dead loss with tools, got everything crooked. Now there were sleazy yellow shutters with clover-shaped holes in them.

Life in that house now seemed like a dream, or a television play he'd once seen. He stood staring over the gate until a woman came out in the garden and glanced at him questioningly. Just as well. He moved on, his eyes itching. Funny, he couldn't remember Dad's face. But he could remember the Volkswagen, the green upholstery, and the bright glitter of the line he had scratched right around the car with a twenty-cent piece.

Well, Dad was gone, he and the old Volks in one blinding flare because of some crummy drunken driver. And now Mum had married Dr Aarons and would be away in England for two years.

Gideon had felt very badly about this. He didn't know why. He just felt insulted, as if his mother had in the crudest manner made it clear that he and Ludie were not enough for her. The way he felt, the revelation of his vulnerability to unhappiness just because he liked his mother, had been the direst shock to Gideon. He made up his mind that he would never be caught that way again. He would learn how to be offhand with everybody. And icy with some, such as Valentine and Birrell Hobby. There'd be no more of the junior school Donk stuff from Hobby, either. Cool Hand Gideon, that would be his line from now on.

In Gideon's suitcase there were several letters from his mother, the latest from the village in the Hebrides where the doctor had gone on exchange. Gideon had read them all, often. But as yet he hadn't replied. Aside from the fact that he just couldn't bring himself to write to her, he didn't know what to say. And the longer he went without answering, the more difficult the whole thing became.

He was melancholy and out of sorts with himself, and he didn't care that Ludie and Valentine knew it.

He lay on his bed, looking out into the gloomy crimson of the western sky. Big planes moved slowly across it, like gilded blowflies, already low on their approach to the airport. The sound of the city was a grinding roar, punctuated by recurrent sudden snarls as the traffic moved off at green lights.

There wasn't much noise in Cassia Court. On their floor, the top, there were eight units, all but one occupied by business people. They rushed out before eight o'clock, rushed back about six-thirty. But even after that time the subdued sound of a mixmaster, a radio, the clonk of the garbage-chute cover near the stairs was all that let you know that other humans lived beyond your own walls. There was really no one around during the day except the Old Mouse, a thin old woman in 306. Gideon had met her a couple of times in the lift, but she hadn't bothered to say good day, so he hadn't either.

He hadn't noticed what she looked like. All old ladies looked the same. But Ludie called her the Old Mouse, so he expected she looked like one. Valentine disapproved of this nickname. It was the only time Gideon had seen him a little short with Ludie. He said the old lady deserved the use of her name, Mrs Someone, because she had human dignity like everyone else. Valentine, an authentic wet, had a heart that overflowed for everyone and everything. Whales, birds, polluted rivers, criminals. You name it, he could blubber for it.

Now Gideon thought that there must be a way up to the roof of Cassia Court. He'd have a look at the city with his binoculars, see the names of ships in the Harbour, numbers on planes. Even a flying-saucer, for in spite of what had happened at Hobbys' he still believed in the probability of such things.

He expected the roof to be a bare, windswept place, but instead it had all kinds of junk on it, packing cases, dead plants in rusty tins, a big padlocked cupboard where the caretaker presumably kept his paint pots and so on, a tall TV aerial whining in the wind.

Gideon crouched behind the packing cases, and rested the binoculars on the parapet. It was freezing cold up on the roof, but interesting. To the south he could see as far as Botany Bay. Maybe as far as Parramatta to the west. He fancied that the soft smudge of amber fog lying all along the western skyline came from the industrial suburbs that lay like thirty-two kilometres of solid cement between Sydney and Parramatta. As far as the eye could see, Cassia Court was surrounded by identical, and nearly identical high-rise buildings – balconied spaghetti packets called, Gideon imagined, Grevillea Court, Waratah Court, Frangipani Court and so on. At night they looked like slabs of illuminated honeycomb but now they seemed exactly like some vast industrial installation. Nothing to do with humans at all.

Nearby there was nothing to be seen with the binoculars except housewives squeezing kids into pyjamas or getting their husband's dinners ready.

Away out through the Heads he picked up a large oil

tanker, small as a log in those hydrangea-blue waters, tossing up first one end and then the other, and flying what he thought was a Greek flag.

Suddenly the little door at the top of the stairs opened, and out came the Old Mouse. Naturally Gideon didn't need any boring yap from her, so he hunched down and waited for her to do whatever she was going to do, and then nick off.

She was wearing a winter coat and had a dark scarf over her white hair. She carried a shopping basket that seemed heavy.

Not seeing Gideon, she walked briskly past him to the parapet and stepped up on a box which lay just below it.

Gideon wondered what the hell the old duck was going to look at. Then, rather stiffly, she levered herself up on the parapet and jumped over the edge.

Gideon felt as though all the blood had drained out of his legs and was lying there on the concrete in actual pools. His breath caught somewhere in his throat like a lump of cold Clag. He couldn't see properly for a moment. Then sight came back to him, everything very bright, the edges of things red as embers from the vanished sun. And one of those things was the Old Mouse, coming back through the air to touch down on the roof feet first, like a penguin on a beach.

'Bum!' she said angrily as she passed him, slapping raindrops off herself.

Gideon now saw that big round drops were falling on the roof.

She zizzed into the stair doorway and vanished.

Gideon had often heard of people shaking like a leaf. Now it was his turn, vibrating all over as if he were using an invisible jackhammer. He didn't know whether to be sick or not. He leaned over and hung his mouth open but nothing happened.

He thought, 'Somehow I've flipped.'

Presently the old woman came out of the door again. She had put on a dark raincoat and fastened under her chin a rain hat of evil design. She zizzed past him again and, without even the slightest hesitation, clambered up on the parapet and plunged out into space.

She vanished into the golden mist of the smog. Gideon stayed on the roof until darkness came, but she didn't return.

He couldn't eat his dinner. Not that it was any loss, as Valentine had cooked it – misshapen little rissoles reeling alcoholically around the plate, and some kind of cauliflower scunge befouled with sauce that tasted like car exhaust.

Ludie was anxious. 'Feel all right, Gid? Not coming down with anything?'

Valentine looked at him benevolently with his soft eyes. Gideon could have poked them out. He mumbled something and escaped.

He went to bed early, for he just had to think things over. Lying there, staring at the ruby on top of the Bridge, seeing a searchlight fingering the invisible clouds, he went over it again.

First of all, he hadn't turned into a kook. He had seen that Old Mouse fly. Twice. Thirty floors! Allowing three metres to each floor – but perhaps there was even more space between them? Otherwise one person's floor would be the down-below's actual ceiling which didn't sound right. Okay then, say three and a half metres per floor. That was over a hundred metres high. And that old woman had confidently stepped off, into nothing but air.

But how?

A witch? Was it true that there were witches?

'What *are* you?' Gideon said scornfully to himself. Suddenly, like a bang on the head, it struck him. She must be an alien.

Gideon had always considered it preposterous that people should think life-forms from other worlds should be purple jellies, or spiky things, or even worse, bare old brains in basins, blupping away with fantastic power.

Any alien clever enough to travel from say, one of the planets of Alpha Centaurus, would be clever enough to create a disguise that looked exactly like a human. An alien, if it were to get anywhere at all in research, or conquest, or just plain monstering, would have to be to all intents and purposes a human. But of course underneath he would retain his other-worldly powers.

'She flew because she hadn't an idea that I was watching,' concluded Gideon. Scared triumph filled him. He had spotted the beast from outer space masquerading as the most harmless of human beings, an old lady. But she had said 'Bum!', just like any old lady who remembered the word from her childhood as a naughty one. An old lady forced to come back for her raincoat, and grumpy about it. Would an alien really go to such lengths, when it believed itself unobserved? He had ideas of going to the police, or ringing up a government department perhaps. But whom would you ask for, and what would you say when you got them? 'Excuse me, I saw an old lady fly off the top of Cassia Court.' On your way, creep, I'm a busy man. Or: Don't fret about it, chum, but if you see any little green men let us know at once. You nut.

The whole thing was so disturbing he could scarcely think straight. One minute he thought he really must have gone crazy; the next that the Old Mouse had hypnotised him in some way.

She had come back safely, anyway. The next morning he had seen her jamming some garbage into the chute as normally as could be.

A letter came to Ludie from their mother, and Ludie read it out, including the piece about being anxious because of Gideon's long silence.

Ludie said, 'You rat, Gid. I had a feeling you weren't writing. Why not?'

Gideon shrugged, coolly.

'He'll write when he's ready, Lu,' put in Valentine reasonably.

Ludie took no notice, but burst out, 'If you feel badly about her marrying again, then you ought to come out with it, Gid. Be open. You can't imagine how much better you'll feel,' she added, with sincerity that nearly zonked him with embarrassment.

Valentine said, 'Oh, leave the boy alone, Lu. He'll work things out his own way.'

This was so exactly what Gideon was resentfully thinking that he could have murdered Valentine. Murder being out of the question, he sat there unseeingly watching TV and mentally running over all the various instruments of torture he had invented for his brother-in-law. There was a fabulously sharp circular razor-blade thing, which could be concealed in Valentine's prehistoric Beatle cap. At a given moment, preferably in the middle of Pitt Street, it went into action and scalped him.

There was the Optical Distorting Fluid which, when rubbed on the inside of Valentine's repulsive glasses, made him see everything upside-down. Or sideways?

There was the Electronic Scorpion which Gideon was still working on. Its destination was inside Valentine's incomparably grotty nightshirt. At this moment Ludie was massaging the furry back of her husband's neck. What *are* you? he silently appealed, and contempt nearly choked him.

That evening when he was on the roof, shivering, angry at everybody and everything, he saw the Old Mouse returning home, outlined against the city lights like a woolly shadow, landing neatly but with a brief curse as she knocked her foot against the parapet. She felt around in her basket, fetched out a little torch and scuttled confidently across to the stair door. She had the basket again, but it seemed empty. Gideon plainly saw her face as she entered the door; it was white and crumpled with fatigue.

In that moment he was perfectly sure she was just a weary old woman and not an alien. The relief was so great that he went to bed and slept like a log. Next morning he awakened with the firm intention of going to see the Old Mouse and getting the truth out of her.

That was easier resolved than done. It took Gideon most of the day to screw up his nerve sufficiently to go and knock on the Old Mouse's door. By the time she opened it, his whole middle had begun to quiver. Seen up close the Old Mouse wasn't so much like an Old Mouse as an old bandicoot. Without a bandicoot's

meekness, though. This was a suspicious, hostile bandicoot with eyes like date-stones. She wore a tennis eyeshade and a cardigan that hoicked up at the back. The
date-stones flicked him a glance from head to foot.

'Yes? What do you want?' She had an old lady voice
with a crack in it.

'I'm from 301,' he began, but she cut in.

'Got a complaint, have you? Radio on too loud?
Washing dishes too late at night? Out with it.'

'Well, no,' said Gideon. Around his collarbones he
felt a blush heating up.

'Go away then,' snapped the old lady. 'Pest!'

She shut the door. Without warning anger seized
Gideon. It was almost like having a fit, he thought afterwards, nothing actually to do with him at all. He
thumped on the door, holding his face close to it as if for
two cents he'd gnaw his way through.

At the tenth thump the door whisked open and he
almost fell inside. 'You just listen to me!' he said in a
loud grating voice that amazed him. The old lady
seemed smaller than ever. She came up to Gideon's chin.
He felt huge and tottery and half-mad.

'Please,' he muttered.

'Speak your piece,' ordered the old lady, pushing up
her eyeshade. She did not look afraid or even startled.
Just wary.

'I saw you,' he blurted. 'On the roof.' It seemed
impossible to get the rest of it out without stuttering.
But he did.

'Flying.'

'Big deal,' commented the Old Mouse. She began to
close the door. Gideon got his foot in the way.

'You've got to talk to me!' he cried.

'No, I haven't. Buzz off.'

The audacity of this struck Gideon dumb. While he was thinking what to do or say, the lift whined and clacked into view and Valentine stepped out.

'Oh, Mr Pozzi,' quavered the old woman, suddenly becoming a hundred years old and not a bit well. 'Your nephew here wants something but I can't quite make out what it is.'

'Brother-in-law,' corrected Valentine mildly. He came forward with his understanding face on. 'What's it about, Gid?'

Gideon mumbled something about finding a page of a letter in the passage. It sounded half-witted the moment he said it. Valentine was puzzled. 'But what made you think that Mrs Oliver . . . ?'

'Thought I saw her drop it,' gabbled Gideon, bursting with fury.

'Such a kind lad,' said Mrs Oliver, looking with a baffled smile from one to the other and now at least 110. Shaking her head, still smiling, she gently closed her door.

'Where's this page, Gid?' asked Valentine. 'Maybe I . . .'

'Blew away,' said Gideon. 'Out the window. Gone.'

He walked quickly to Unit 301, Valentine following. Fortunately the lift appeared, and Ludie shot out, up to the chin in supermarket bags, almost falling. One of her Dr Scholls had slipped off, and went down again in the lift.

'Oh, damn,' said Ludie. 'Get it for me, will you, Val? I've got to have a shower, I'm whacked, what a day.'

She stretched out for a kiss. They began one of their chin fights, which as a rule nearly dropped Gideon through the floor with embarrassment. But now he welcomed the contest and escaped into the unit, knowing that Valentine would forget about the letter and the Old Mouse.

The shameless deceit of Mrs Oliver hardened Gideon's resolution.

'Oh, Mr Pozzi!' he repeated to himself, in sarcastic imitation. 'Such a kind lad. The old monster!'

He was determined to catch her out if it was the last thing he did.

'Right,' he thought. 'We have here an old lady who can, somehow, fly. She's not going to fly in broad daylight. No way. People would see her. She doesn't want publicity. Neither is she going to rocket off in the night. She might bang into the arch of the Bridge, or high-tension powerlines or something.'

He worked out that Mrs Oliver's prime flying time must be just at rush hour, when practically no one would be gazing up in the air, and there was still plenty of light for her to nip off to wherever she went. Probably, coming home, she flew low to pick up the reflected glare from the city, and not so late that there were many hazardous dark patches. The next time Mrs Oliver went up to the roof with her heavy basket she found Gideon sitting on the packing cases and looking cool. She was disconcerted. With triumph Gideon saw a thin, thin flush creep up her papery cheek.

'Good afternoon, Mrs Oliver,' he said, with a civility so well done he might have been an actor.

She came straight up to him and barked, 'Don't you bug me, boy!'

He barked back. 'You don't own the roof. I can come up here if I like.'

She turned right around and went downstairs again. Gideon was not dismayed. He knew what he would do in her place. So he went behind the packing cases and waited. Sure enough, in twenty minutes or so, she reappeared, looking relieved as she swept a glance around the roof.

Just as she stepped up on the box below the parapet, Gideon slipped out and said: 'Good afternoon, Mrs Oliver.'

She whipped around, hesitated a moment, glaring at him. Then she said, 'Blow you!' and took off with such force that she got caught in the updraft between Cassia Court and an even taller building diagonally across the road. She had a panicky flapping moment or two before she got her balance and swept away in a long curve into the dimming west.

Gideon was shaken. He had thought she was going to fall. At the same time there was an ache inside him. How fabulous it must be, the great city beside the darkening sea, the buildings like ruined towers, creeping or rushing brilliant things everywhere, cars and buses and spangled snakes of electric trains. The Opera House like a cluster of settling white butterflies. And all wasted on an old lady like a bandicoot.

When he returned to the unit, Ludie was banging plates around, and Valentine was morosely pretending to take notes from a textbook. Gideon could see they'd had an argument, and he felt sure it was about him.

All through the meal Ludie was silent, eating with her front teeth, which was what Gideon did himself when he felt upset. Ludie was a zappy girl, but now she looked like a half-starved cat. Even her hair fell over her face in dismal clumps. He had a brief pang, as if she were some pathetic kid. But he had no time for Ludie's troubles, he was too involved in the astonishing thing that had happened to him. Wild excitement gripped him. He had come face to face with wonder, and he knew it might never happen again. The explanation of Mrs Oliver's talent was insignificant compared with the fact of Mrs Oliver's existence.

He felt he knew the correct line to take. He knew how he'd feel if he could fly and some person kept idling around staring. Outraged. Yes, and scared, too, in case they told, and he was never allowed to do it again. There was bound to be some kind of traffic law or council ordinance about airborne individuals and the hazards they caused.

So he just sat around on the roof looking intelligent but aloof, while the old woman got used to him. At first she gave him evil ratty glances, then she ignored him, and he sensed that a wary truce was developing. He moved cautiously towards an acquaintanceship. He could not call it friendship, for how could anyone be friends with anyone so old, even if spectacularly gifted?

He made the first move by approaching her and saying, 'You don't have to worry about me, Mrs Oliver. Saying anything, I mean.'

She did not smile, or thank him, merely peered at him glumly. However, he knew that she was grateful.

'Good,' she said. 'Cheerybye then,' and jumped out into space.

She had this old-fashioned manner of speaking. Sometimes she said 'hurroo' for a change.

The Old Mouse and Gideon progressed to sparse, grouchy conversation. Once or twice Gideon did something for her, in a brutally offhand way. He put a washer on a tap, and took the hinges off a wardrobe door which had stuck, unstuck it, and put the hinges neatly back.

'You did that pretty well,' she said grudgingly. He grunted.

'I can't cook for nuts,' she said. 'But I got some sandwiches at the deli. Feel like a bite?'

He looked at the sandwiches, thick chicken slices and well-dried salad.

'No beetroot?'

She shook her head. 'I hate the rotten stuff. The way your teeth sink into it!'

'With a squog.'

'That's it.'

They ate. She didn't ask his age, what college he attended, whether he hated boarding school, or what he wanted to be when he was older. Gideon could see that she didn't care a dry spit about any of these things. It gave him a wonderful sense of privacy.

Cautiously he asked a little about her flying, ready to pull back his horns like a snail at the first sign of a rebuff. How did she find out she could fly?

'I just thought I might be able to, so I jumped off. Bit clumsy at first, kept turning head downwards. Alarming, that was. Got the hang of it after a bit, though. Everyone can fly. I'm certain of it.'

'Why do people fall then,' queried Gideon, 'when they jump off cliffs and things?'

'They expect to. So they do. I know better. So do you, now. Well if that's all you're going to eat, clear out.'

Another time he dared to ask her where she went, every other day and always in the same direction. He expected to be told to mind his own business but he wasn't.

'An old fellow,' she explained vaguely. 'Bedbound. Cranky old buzzard. No one left to give him a hand. I go over on those days when the district nurse or Meals on Wheels don't call. Flying's quick and handy. It would take me an hour and a half with public transport. Hate public transport.'

'He must be a great friend of yours,' ventured Gideon.

She looked surprised. 'Friend? No, never cared for him much. Acquaintance of my late husband's really. But I can't leave him alone as long as I can help him out, can I? Besides, he's the only person left who calls me Enid.'

'Why does he call you that?' asked Gideon, uncomprehending.

'Because it's my name, you clot,' she snapped. 'Did you think I was christened Mrs?'

Gideon thought about that bit quite a lot. It must be creepy not ever to be called by your name. He tried it. Not Gideon but Mr Bray. Grandpa Bray. Or Old Man Bray. That old fool Bray? Even (and he remembered how Valentine had chided Ludie about the Old Mouse) the Old Something. It was fantastic that he himself should ever come to resemble an animal, even a nice cute one. But he looked in the glass to see if it were possible.

He stared carefully at his face. There seemed to be quite a touch of the fish about it, round eyes, small neat mouth, everything coming to a point. The Old Fish? Worse, the Old Flounder?

The idea spooked him. He put two fingers in his mouth and tried to stretch it.

The marvellous view behind him could be seen in the mirror, starry smudges and blots, and luminous raspberries and green plums. He looked at its reflection for a while. She had to go out tonight, Mrs Oliver, amongst the city constellations, and would come home a little late with an exhausted look, as though she'd nearly drowned. The old man she went to tend was ill; he might have to go to hospital, but he was convinced it would be for the last time, and he was battling it.

'He's right, of course,' she said that morning, in her staccato way, like someone spitting pips. 'Once they get you down, it's nankipoo for you.'

Gideon was beginning to understand her archaic speech.

'Well, you want to be careful,' he said. 'You oughtn't to be flying at night.'

'Who says?' she challenged.

'I say,' said Gideon. 'You might collide with a plane in the dark.'

'Don't be dotty!' But an unexpected smile was in her eyes. She said broodingly, 'That's the way I'd like to go. Heart attack in mid-air. Swoop! Crash! Spare the crows, look at that, old lady fell from heaven like a shooting star! Poor old soul, she's had it, she's . . .'

'Nankipoo,' suggested Gideon.

She began to laugh. Gideon laughed too, because it was the first time he'd heard her laugh, and it was a funny noise. Suddenly she stopped.

'What I wouldn't like,' she said, 'would be to get tangled in one of those aerials that stick up like fishing rods from the high roofs. You never see the damned things until you're nearly on them. I've had a close shave or two . . .' She stopped, and said gruffly, 'Hate to get caught and dangle in one of them until daylight, especially in winter.'

'I wish you wouldn't fly at night, then,' said Gideon. In dismay he heard his voice assume a dovelike tone. He might have been Valentine pleading with Ludie to be careful going down the stairs in her health shoes. He was quite relieved when Mrs Oliver yapped, 'Mind your own business!'

'Ta ra, then,' he said.

'Ta ra!' she said, so peevishly that he knew she was genuinely scared of those TV aerials on the high-risers.

But still, tonight she would go out there. Why? To help keep an unlovable old nuisance of a man out of hospital.

'Might be the best place for him, after all,' Gideon could hear his own voice of a few days ago.

'He wants to die in his own home, and why shouldn't he?' demanded the Old Mouse. 'Nobody's going to take away his freedom of choice while I'm around.'

Suddenly Gideon saw Valentine's beard in the mirror. He had been so abstracted that at first he stared at it, this soft, colourless puff, wondering what it was that was blotting out the cityscape. Then he saw the glasses. Valentine was standing near the door, looking calm and holy.

'Come on out, friend,' he said. 'Talk to me.'

Gideon's blood froze. This was Ludie's night out at an enamelling class. No way was he going to spend the evening talking sincerely with someone who addressed him as 'friend'. Valentine was on about something, and Gideon was trapped.

He put on his most churlish look. Ideas rushed around his mind like bolting horses. Meeting someone to go to a movie? Sick? Study even? No good.

Valentine said, peering at Gideon's chin with odious

sympathy, 'Got a yerk, have you?'

Of its own volition Gideon's hand flew up to cover an insignificant bump on his chin. Valentine said, 'Not to worry, old son. Sign of maturity.'

Gideon had never heard such a grotty statement, not even from the college chaplain. He flung himself out into the living room, down like a rug in front of the TV. He turned the set on. He could feel his pimple swelling like a red-hot peanut. Valentine said plaintively, 'Fair go, Gid. We have to talk sometime.'

Gideon mumbled, turned down the sound.

Valentine said, 'Ludie thinks I ought to. But I'm for non-interference. I believe *profoundly* in freedom.'

He dripped on for a while like this, while Gideon stared smoulderingly at the carpet, felt his pimple growing, and in a burst of fury and genius finished the Electronic Scorpion. He tipped its sting with a culture of a rare virus – Blue Pedal and Digital Fungus disease, it produced – and secreted it in the pocket of Valentine's nightshirt.

'You're not coming in clear, Dad,' said Gideon.

He was not an insolent boy. He believed that insolence showed lack of control of a situation. Not Cool Hand Gideon's scene at all. But this time his words came out with a vulgar rasp. Valentine caught it and, disconcerted, blushed. It was as if Gideon had called him a capitalist or kangaroo-hunter.

He blurted 'Don't you patronise me! You kids, you think you own the earth. Well, let me tell you – ' Here he stopped, shocked. Quickly he closed his eyes and began to breathe in a mystic rhythm. Gideon got his face into a sneer ready for the moment when Valentine rejoined him.

'Right,' said Valentine, opening up. 'Skip all that. What I'm saying is that it upsets Ludie that you seem to be hostile towards your mother. Really upsets her. She frets.'

'None of your affair,' ground out Gideon. He stared at the TV where a big face was waggling its lips and twitching its eyes. A hand came up and winsomely poked a pencil into the face's dimple. Gideon wished passionately that the pencil point would go right in and get jammed.

Valentine reached over and turned off the picture. His hand looked nervous, and his voice had a pleading note. Gideon gave him a cruelly hard stare that further unsettled him.

'It is my business, Gid, if it upsets Ludie. I mean, for her sake, won't you try to get things straight about your Mum? Your Mum has to make her own decisions, live her own life. If she hurt you, that's not what she meant to do –'

Gideon made some excellent retching noises. Valentine turned a darker red. 'Okay then, work it out for yourself, you dumb – oh, what's the use? I *told* Ludie, there's no way, I said, he's too infantile to – '

Gideon jumped up to walk away, but Valentine blocked him, almost shouting, 'You're not going till I've said a few words about the way you treat Ludie, poor little thing, so warm and kind, but you never show affection, even interest in her. When do you ask about her work, or her stupid enamel ash-trays, or anything else that shows she's got a life of her own? Meal times! They bug me, man, they bug me one hundred per cent. You sitting there, not talking to her, just sitting there pushing your food around and putting on your fruit-bat face.'

'Belt up!' bawled Gideon, and he rushed blindly past his brother-in-law, intending to get into his room. But when he slammed the door he was back in the bathroom, trapped there until Valentine went to bed or dropped dead or something.

He was so mad he didn't know what to do. All the things that had bothered him lately, and a lot that had bothered him years ago, and he had thought forgotten, all rushed together and hit him in a bewildering flood, so that he felt actually freaked out. He just leaned against the window, blowing hard through his nose, until the flood subsided. Then he felt empty, and freezing cold.

He saw the lights obscured for a moment, and glimpsed the dark bundled shape of Mrs Oliver, soaring up past the parapet of the high-rise across the street and vanishing into fumes and cloud. Gideon thought, 'There's going to be a storm, she shouldn't be going out, silly old twit.' But he couldn't keep his mind on it. He sat down on the edge of the dwarf corner bath.

He thought, 'I'm bloody miserable.'

It was queer realising that he realised it. Like looking in a mirror to see his reflection in a mirror. It came to him then that when you're a small kid you don't realise much. You just are. But the time comes when you know what you're feeling, you can describe it, or take steps to change things. According to the Old Mouse you could, anyway. Naturally, she could just be talking, as adults so often talked, just streaming away at the mouth because of their primitive dread of silence. But the Old Mouse simply did not care what he or anyone else thought of her and her ideas. It was unlikely that she'd feed him the party line just for the sake of it.

A splatter of rain flung itself in the window. Thunder

mumbled threateningly in the west. An endless hour
went by. It was dreary in the bathroom and there was a
funny smell of wet towels and soggy soap. To pass the
time Gideon gazed into the glass and tried to look like a
fruit bat. But who could? Probably Valentine had never
seen one. Gideon had, at Hobbys' place. Tiny sparky
eyes and a squashed devil's snout, hanging upside down
in a mango tree. Remembering that made him think of
all the things that had worried him at Hobbys'. He tried
to turn his thoughts away but he was so dragged out he
didn't have the energy.

Not Birrell's snickering little sisters and all the
'secrets' they seemed to have about him. They were a
matched set of uglies, but only kids, after all. Not Mrs
Hobby, and her freaky questions about his family, what
his father had done, how he had died, his mother's new
husband, his branch of medicine, and so on, until he had
said, 'Why do you want to know?' which made her
congeal and scarcely ever speak to him again.

There was the wine served with dinner, which Birrell
drank as if it were Coke, but which rose straight to
Gideon's head, so that when he rose from the table his
knees gave way under him. And not being able to ride.

'How could I?' thought Gideon in silent protest to the
bathroom walls. 'Living in the city. Not everyone can
ride, why was I expected to? Going on and on about it,
as if . . . as if . . .' In-jokes. Baffling remarks at which
everybody roared except Gideon. And Birrell's Franken-
stein Uncle Kev, a fat nutter with a white Volvo softtop
and a red varnished face. Finding out that Gideon was a
science-fiction buff, and had a dozen SF paperbacks
beside his bed, he had christened Gideon Captain Snurgle and kept asking if he were off on the next rocket to

Venus. Well, that was all right, bearable, anyway, but Uncle Kev would keep on rubbishing the original ideas that were found so profusely in SF. For the sake of his self-respect, Gideon couldn't let that pass. He protested, 'Practically every big step forward in science was written about in SF years and years ago – laser beams, and space platforms, and interplanetary travel, and antigrav –'

Halfway through he was drowned out by Uncle Kev's big dumb ho-ho-hos. So he got up and walked out. It was either that or tell the old nerd to shut his face.

'Give my regards to all those six-armed popsies on Mars, Captain Snurgle,' yelled Uncle Kev after him, and everyone laughed as if he were a Marx brother. Even Birrell.

Birrell, who keenly read all Gideon's SF books, and had even developed a theory of his own about Time being spiral instead of a plain old line; when it was properly worked out they were going to call it Hobby's Law.

Yet here he was, howling at Gideon, not because he found him laughable, but because he had to run with the crowd, be on the side of the majority. And when Gideon thought about it, that had been Birrell's line right through the holiday.

The thing wounded Gideon out of all proportion to its importance. His friend had betrayed him.

'He should have stuck up for me, and his own ideas, too,' thought Gideon.

It was queer how, after that, Birrell's very face seemed to be different. At school Gideon had always thought of him as being sharp looking, bright. But at home he had a mean birdy look, like a skinny, diminished Uncle Kev.

It was mostly Birrell's treachery that had spoiled all

the good things about the holiday at Hobbys' place. But now Gideon understood something else. It was pretty weird to understand it in a bathroom, with Valentine patiently rapping on the door and asking why didn't he come out to watch the soccer replay, but he did.

Birrell had found him an embarrassment. To Birrell's way of thinking Gideon had failed him because somehow he had turned out to be the butt of the family jokes, and not taking it well. He had said as much, once or twice.

'You should have passed it off, not let Uncle Kev get to you.'

'Why should he want to get to me, you tell me that,' replied Gideon, but of course Birrell had no answer.

After the rain had been shushing down past the bathroom window for some time, Gideon heard Valentine thumping around in the bedroom. He tapped on the door, called, 'Gid, I'm just going to meet Ludie with her coat and the umbrella. Gid?'

'I heard you. Right?' answered Gideon sharply. He thought he heard Valentine sigh as he turned away.

After the lift descended, Gideon went along to see if Mrs Oliver had come home. But her unit was dark and silent.

Aimlessly he prowled around his own place, looking at the bookcase of planks set on bricks. Valentine's textbooks, Ludie's thrillers, *National Geographic*s belonging to them both. They were both mad to travel.

One magazine was folded over at an article on the Hebrides. Mull. Iona. Guys in sweaters that looked as if they were knitted of frayed rope. Seawalls, seabirds and wet rocks.

Looking at those windswept scenes, Gideon thought

for the first time that things must be pretty weird for Ludie, too. Worse, perhaps, for she had Valentine to put up with. It was even possible, he thought with surprise, that their mother didn't feel too good without Ludie and him. He slammed shut the *Geographic* and put it back on the pile. It was now ten-thirty. Valentine and Ludie were probably having a cup of coffee somewhere. Gideon went along to Mrs Oliver's unit to check again. No sign of life.

He thought, 'The weather's so terrible she probably stayed over at the old man's flat. What else could she do?'

Ludie's unit was as cold as the Arctic. It seemed as small as a kennel, furnished with makeshifts. Filled with melancholy Gideon mooched around. He thought perhaps he was hungry, and looked in the refrigerator. There was a greasy brown thing lying dead on a dish. Gideon was curious enough to poke at it. He thought it was a fried banana. Shuddering, he put on his raincoat, took his binoculars and went up on the roof. The rain had stopped temporarily. The air had a prickling intensity about it, as if electrified. The city looked fabulous, canals of flowing lights, greenish and ghost-blue stars and planets. Whole galaxies that were the eastern suburbs. Dim Magellanic clouds far to the south and west, Wollongong perhaps. Penrith. A storm stood on the rampart of the Blue Mountains, just poised, waiting, intermittently hammering down lightning into the plains below. And even further away, over Bathurst perhaps, or the Hunter Valley, was a colossal cloud mass, black as coal. Deep within it was a dazzling pulse that illuminated other spectral shapes that were swift clouds chasing across the sky.

Gideon leaned over the parapet, saw straight down the precipitous side of Cassia Court a taxi pull in, and Ludie and Valentine emerge into the light. He watched the doll-sized figures hurry towards shelter, Valentine's arm around Ludie.

Gideon knew he couldn't go down to the unit right away. He didn't suppose that Valentine would force another confrontation. He would be ashamed that he'd lost his temper, tossed around abuse. That wasn't his style and he'd feel humiliated that he'd behaved like a human instead of Father Christmas. The truth was that he, Gideon, didn't want to see Ludie and Valentine contented just with each other. He was on the outside of them, just as he was on the outside of his mother and Dr Aarons.

He'd also been on the outside of the Hobbys. He understood now that they were the kind of people who thought that everyone on the outside of their little group didn't amount to much. He remembered Mum Hobby, pulling her wealth and her social position around her shoulders like a coat. Just as if she were chilly inside and didn't know what else to do about it.

Mrs Oliver wasn't like that. She wasn't a warm lady like, say, Ludie. She was sharp, almost spiteful. Snip snap, mind what you say or I'll have your nose off. She wasn't your usual adult; she did not urge or advise or get your back up by turning benignant. She was just herself, take her or leave her. She did not need to be inside with anyone.

'She's a really free person,' thought Gideon. It wasn't even being able to fly that made her a free person. He knew that Mrs Oliver believed that everyone could fly.

But once she had had to make the decision to find out if she could really fly. Had that made her free?

When he asked Mrs Oliver this, she had nodded. 'That's it. Not the decision alone. Choices – heavens, we make them all the time. But every choice brings consequences that may be disagreeable for ourselves or other people. A truly free choice – well, that's one where you're prepared to take what's coming, good or bad.' She paused a moment and then said, as if to herself, 'That's where freedom is.' It had come into Gideon's mind then that she was thinking of the many dangers of flying. But she had chosen to dare them, and for a person whom she didn't like very much.

There was a splash of rain, and Gideon retreated under the shelter of the stair doorway, leaning there idly sweeping the big sky with the binoculars. Though they were not night-glasses, he could see a surprising amount after dark with them. Once he had seen Mars rising – a hard, glistening copper disc.

Now he found a fuzzy yellow cloud out at sea, which resolved itself into a tourist liner, all portholes blazing, taking on the pilot. He tried to catch the lightning, but it was too swift, too dazzling, and left him half-blinded. He was so lonely and wretchedly cold that he almost enjoyed not being able to see properly. He told himself how horrible it must be to be blind, but he couldn't care.

His stomach gave a puling little chirrup, and he realised that he was sick with hunger. Soon he'd have to go down and face Ludie and Valentine just for the sake of having something to eat. He waited till all the lights became sharp once more, and, just to put off the moment when he'd have to go downstairs, he took up the binoculars and swept the wet world. There were moonbows around the streetlights. Lights on top of buildings blinked as shadows of shuddering flagpoles passed across them.

Then he saw Mrs Oliver. At first he couldn't believe it. There couldn't actually be a person caught high in the staywires of a TV aerial on a building a street, maybe two streets away. The glasses kept losing the target; his eyes felt as if they were dropping out of his head.

Then he found the right roof again, saw the dark bundle flapping weakly. A hat or something fell off and he saw white hair in the deceitful light. Lightning zipped across the city like a photo-flash, and he saw the bundle detach itself from the rigging and fall five metres, maybe more, to the roof below. He lost the field again, fiddled around, at last picked up the shape feebly moving, trying to get up, collapsing, being still.

The thing Mrs Oliver dreaded, dreaded so much that she couldn't speak of it properly, had happened. She was disabled up there, on a murderously cold night, with the rain lashing down, and no chance of her being found till morning. Perhaps not even then, for who would go up on the roof of a high-rise in this weather? Nobody knew where she was but Gideon. But he could be there in three minutes. He rushed at the parapet. The wind whooshed up from the street, full of wet and anger. It blew him back, deafened him with street sounds and its own sounds, howls and wails and whistles. But he clung to the parapet, jumped up on Mrs Oliver's wooden box, lifted his arms, and knew she was right, he could fly.

It was as if his whole body was filled with cells of air. He sensed, like a bird, that the rivers of wind would buoy him up as strongly as if they were rivers of water.

Then he glanced down the glittering cliff of Cassia Court, and the terrible canyon speared up into his eyes with its lights and depth and emptiness.

He did not think, 'I can't, I won't.' He felt it. Yet at the same moment his whole body longed to be away from the parapet, out amongst the tumult of the air. It was his mind that made the choice, turned him away, crying, 'No, Mrs Oliver, no, no.'

He clattered down the stairs, punched the button of the lift, again, again, though it was already ascending. The door slid open and he barged in, not aware for a second or two that the lift already held Valentine.

His brother-in-law stared at him, stupefied.

Gideon kept saying, 'No, no, Mrs Oliver' until he saw Valentine, then he stopped. But he went on saying it inside.

Valentine said, 'What's the matter? I was just coming to see where you . . . Gid, what do you mean about Mrs Oliver, you're as pale as a ghost. Speak to me, damn it!' yelled Valentine.

The lift gently stopped on the ground floor, and Gideon rushed past Valentine. The front door was already snicked for the night; he could not open it. Valentine caught up with him and grabbed him.

'Gideon, cool it! Tell me what's wrong.'

'Mrs Oliver,' said Gideon. 'She's up on the roof of a building. Hurt. I saw her through my binoculars.'

Valentine stared at him as if he'd blown his mind.

'Which building?'

'I don't know, you idiot! Over there somewhere!'

He gestured out into the rain. He got the door open and pushed through. He ran as hard as he could towards the street. The rain was punching down, running off

Gideon's hair and down between his neck and his collar. He tore up the street for a hundred metres. There was no one around, just cars hissing past, a bus groaning around the corner. He halted, the horror of the truth paralysing him. He had said to Valentine that he didn't know which building, and that was true. He cursed himself now for not identifying it by something, number of floors, shape of balconies, something.

He pushed up against a brick wall, trying to get away from the distraction of the rain and the cold, while he thought.

That building on which Mrs Oliver had become marooned was not on this street. It had been behind the cream synthetic-brick slab now directly opposite him. He had been able to see that building because the cream block was slightly lower than Cassia Court – perhaps twenty-eight floors.

The building he wanted was in the street behind. Shaky with relief he raced for the corner. He felt unreal, a mere phantom, Cool Hand Gideon shouting, 'And another thing . . .'

And another thing, if he had been able to see the roof so clearly, that argued that the building was the same height, or just a little less tall than Cassia Court. Cool Hand Gideon came a little closer, reached out a cool, calm hand.

As he turned into the other street, Cool Hand Gideon dwindled and vanished. Six, seven, identical high-rise buildings stood in a geometrical arrangement around a little court, like hobnobbing giants.

He just didn't know where to start, so he started on the first one, going straight up in the lift to the roof. The door was locked on the inside, so he was able to get out on to the windswept waste of bitumen. He saw at once Mrs Oliver wasn't amongst the drenched canvas chairs and the bitty, blown-over tables. He went straight down again. As he crossed the lobby a householder in pyjamas, pottering mysteriously about, asked, 'You looking for someone, son?'

He said no, and hurried out into the rain. In the second building the front door was locked, but Gideon darted into the garage, tried the exit which led to the stairs, and found it open. Mrs Oliver wasn't on that roof, either. It struck him then that he might be able to spot the right roof from this one. He saw two that had the kind of upright, extremely tall TV aerial. So with renewed hope he left the building.

Almost gratefully he saw the tall shape of Valentine, now wearing an anorak and his Beatle cap, peering anxiously up and down the street. Valentine just walked towards him, calling, 'Can I help, mate?'

Gideon said, 'It must be one of those two over there.'

The first one was all locked up for the night, but Valentine put his finger on a button and held it there until the tenant answered furiously, as though he'd been in bed.

'Open the door for me, will you, sir?' barked Valentine. 'We think there's an old woman in trouble on the roof of the building.'

There was a gabble, and the front door opened as if by magic. Gideon and Valentine entered the lift and went upwards. Gideon was still dumbstruck at the authoritative voice that had come out of Valentine's shrunken, wet-cat beard.

'I was being the fuzz, man,' said Valentine, with a kind of sideways grin at Gideon.

They were lucky. There was the TV aerial vibrating in the wind.

There was Mrs Oliver, soaked, unconscious, bones broken – a leg, ribs.

Valentine took care of everything, the police, the ambulance, a doctor. Gideon just crouched beside Mrs Oliver as she lay under his raincoat and Valentine's anorak. He held her frozen wet claw, and kept saying, 'You'll be all right, Mrs Oliver, you'll see.'

But he didn't feel she'd be all right. Wet, she looked like a plucked bird, a small brittle creature too old and too worn out to survive lying around in winter with broken bones and concussion. Ludie rang the hospital early the next morning, but Mrs Oliver was already dead. Gideon put a good face on it for Ludie, who cried, but he saw that Valentine understood how he felt, and he didn't care.

'Gideon was marvellous,' said Ludie. 'It was like some brave act you read about in the papers.'

'Oh, belt up, Lu,' said Gideon.

Valentine thought the extraordinary thing was that Gideon should have spotted Mrs Oliver on the roof.

'Poor old love,' he said. 'She must have been wandering. Old people get that way sometimes. Still, if we had found her sooner she might have lived, I suppose.'

'I guess,' said Gideon, very composed.

Inside he wasn't composed. He went back to college and led an average run of school life, half-fun and half-hell, and no one noticed that he was any different.

Birrell Hobby came back, but took up with a different group of friends, chess-players. Gideon noticed that his face was getting birdier and birdier.

Gideon began to write to his mother, who expressed

no surprise and did not even refer to his long silence, which bugged him somewhat. Then he realised what she was doing, and laughed like a hyena. 'Cool Hand Mum,' he thought.

It took almost six months before he had it all worked out. If he'd been brave enough to fly over to Mrs Oliver as soon as he'd seen her she might have been alive today. However, had he really been too gutless to fly? Because, if so, that was not a free choice.

No, he knew that, although he'd been scared, terrified of that awful canyon of the street, he hadn't been *too* terrified. He could have overcome his fear, as Mrs Oliver must have overcome hers. He had made a free choice, and he had to accept the consequences, of being sorry, maybe all his life. He was bound hand and foot.

He remembered something else she had said. He could hear her wilful, snappy old voice crackling at him, 'Use your loaf, boy. One wrong choice doesn't make you unfree. Life moves along. You can always make another choice.'

'Right,' said Gideon.

'Hurroo, Old Mouse,' he said, after a while. 'Cheerybye, you old rat.'

An old yellow tourer

HARRY PUNCH thought the whole thing a low-down trick of Fate. After weeks of wearing himself to rags pestering his brother to let him have a ride in the old yellow tourer, Malcolm grudgingly said he might come along for a short buzz.

And the first thing Harry set eyes upon was this totally inexplicable spook reflected in the rear-vision mirror.

It hadn't been so awful to look at. It was just not right. And, even worse, not there. It had made the hair on Harry's arms stick straight out like prongs. As a child, he had been inclined towards car sickness and now Malcolm, glimpsing his brother's cheesy face in the mirror (though apparently nothing else), grunted over his shoulder, 'I warn you, Punch, you spew in my car and I'll mince you.'

'Belt up, Punch,' retorted Harry, in a voice so strangled that Malc's girlfriend turned around in the front seat and gave him a quick glance. She was a human kind of person called Laurel and had brothers of her own. The tourer thrummed along like a hoarse old tomcat. Occasionally it uttered a faint yawp and Malc concernedly pulled down his upper lip and did some macho things with the Noah's Ark gears. People stared, even pointed, with awe and admiration, so that Harry, if he hadn't been rigid with shock at the time, would have been as proud as a prince. Malcolm had by no means finished his painstaking work on the old Jowett, but anyone could see that any day now she would be a stately old party that would take the honours at any vintage car rally.

Now and then Harry shot a fast squint at the rear-vision mirror which stuck out on a long arm from the side of the car. Sure enough, the reflection was still there. Of course, it wasn't really. Harry had checked that the instant he got his breath back. The mirror reflected nothing in the car or coming up behind.

It just lived in the mirror, that unknown face did, and Harry hadn't a clue why.

When the short run was over, he was glad to get out of the old yellow tourer. Malc ribbed him a little about that kid stuff of getting squeamy, but Harry let him get away with it, contenting himself with making the usual perfunctory uncivil gesture.

Though they hadn't lived under the same roof for so long, Harry felt that he still understood Malc one hundred per cent. And Harry felt that he, himself, was still Harry. Long ago he had accepted that he was small, commonplace-looking, and frail, cast by fate into the path of every virus in the business. His intention was to become one of those feared, razor-tongued TV comperes before whom tough union reps and State premiers bristled and shook. He was already boss man of the debating society at St Jerome's, and had entered for the New South Wales inter-college debating competition, which he was confident of winning with his tongue nailed down.

The boys' parents had parted more than six years before. The divorce had been an undramatic one. Harry had remained with his mother, but Malcolm, then thirteen, had decided to live with his father.

Vividly Harry remembered the days when Malc had lived with them. He had always been close to his older brother, and when the marriage break-up happened, Harry missed Malc far more than he missed his father. Of course, the brothers saw each other fairly often, four or five times a year, but these meetings had always seemed bogus, a painstaking mock-up of what used to be.

Yet now that Harry had come to live for a while with Dad and Malc and his Dad's new family, things were exactly the way they had been before. He had slipped back into the relationship with Malc as if there had never been a break.

His mother had been transferred for two years to her firm's Paris office, an experience she had always wanted, and it had turned out to be a good thing for all concerned. Harry liked his new school, he enjoyed Sydney's difference from Melbourne, and indeed all systems were go.

Harry's only problem – though indeed it was more of a puzzle – was Dad. Deep down he had this tremendous feeling for him. He supposed it must be love. It was a warmish, swelling feeling. It was queer how this ordinary father had been, in one medium-length lifetime, two different men – both of whom were loved (if that was the word) with equal devotion by his (or their) son Harry.

First of all Dad had had a century or so as an insurance salesman in Melbourne. Sneery blue Porsche, lots of mates, keen on golf and gardening, though actually a bright-pink whistling Dutchman did all the work. And two growing sons whom he thought were kings and didn't care if everyone knew it.

Now he lived in Sydney, running a used-car place. He lived in a hairy, falling-down house in Emily Road, Saltbox Point, which was freaky enough in itself – a long neck of high land where laid-up ships shoved their rusty prows into the jungly backyards, and the front gardens often ran right down to the water's edge on a tidal estuary with decayed boathouses and toppling turpentine piles and bits of old barges sticking up like wooden islets. And all around was the Harbour and the city skyline, diamonded by night and a mixture of wondrousness and fearsome grot by day.

Dad had an eighteenth century Daimler or something with its insides largely composed of polished timber, a baffled but okay new wife called Peke, and a litter of little girls all called Lindy, Mindy or Cindy. The little girls were the furthest thing out about the new Dad scene. Harry couldn't possibly think of them as his half-sisters, though that's what they were. They were just a bunch of Lindies or Mindies or whatever it was. But they all had foxy hair and speckled hazel eyes like Dad. Harry and Malc were dark like their mother. Harry had never thought of his father having any particular coloured hair. His was just a pink head with a patch of greyish-sandy sheen here and there. But here were these new little girls magically reproducing the kind of hair Dad must have had when he was young. It was unreal.

These newcomers consisted of twins of four, another one of three, and then a grub person with a bitter scarlet face protruding from one end of a white woollen bundle. These little chicks looked so alike that Harry couldn't distinguish between them. Except, of course, for the grub which was unlike anything he had ever seen, or ever wanted to see again. He felt dimly benevolent towards them, as if they were pups. Malc just ignored them with the blandness of one ignoring a sunny day. This was characteristic of Malcolm. What he wasn't interested in he didn't even see. He was the same towards Peke.

Peke was a starved-looking girl much younger than Mum. She had hair that just grew, gentle blue eyes and an abstracted look. Before marrying Dad she had been a learner potter, and every window-sill or shelf in the house was adorned with wobbling objects with dribbles of green and blue icing. Occasionally Peke picked up one and mooned over it tenderly, but she did not seem particularly upset when it was accidentally sent flying and smashed by a Cindy or Lindy. Peke got on with living and let other people get on with theirs, which was messy but wonderfully peaceful. Harry had this habit of taking things to eat in bed while he read or studied. He'd put the plate down on the floor and sure as fate he'd step out on top of it next morning. Peke didn't seem to mind, not even when he cut his foot. Without a single yuk she helped him wash the congealed gravy out of the cut, making a fatalistic gesture as though she knew that all inanimate things were hostile, particularly towards the defenceless and innocent.

No, Peke was an all-right lady, though always tired to the point of collapse. She even slept through Dad's monstrous snoring which made Malcolm curse and throw shoes at the wall. Also, Harry liked the careless, mother-cat way she looked after the Mindies. It would have driven his own mother raving bonkers in a day, and in some mysterious manner that pleased Harry as well.

It was Dad who made Harry uneasy. In all kinds of ways poor Dad tried to make contact, though Harry knew that contact was already there. He guessed Dad had read some *Reader's Digest* article – 'Make Contact with Your Son or Else!' He knew, too, that he embarrassed Dad. Perhaps he reminded him of past restless or unhappy years. Of course Harry did his best to put the

71

old man at ease, just as if Dad had been some huge bald new creep at St Jerome's, and Harry himself the prefect told off to see that the new guy settled down according to rules.

One thing was sure, Dad was happy. Serene. Harry was big on serenity, all that gunk. He needed a bland life in order to function at the top of his powers. He could quite see how his fascinating mother (she was cookery editor of a women's magazine but lived on skim milk and rye biscuits herself) could get on Dad's nerves. One surge of essential goofing-off on his part, just to get unjangled, would bring on a bout of briskness. By the time he was eight Harry had learned how to cope with his old lady. She was a stirrer, and had to be kept firmly though civilly in place. But Dad would get either enraged or rattled. Harry found it weird that he could realise so calmly now that his parents did not suit each other, even though each was a really great human being. This Peke, even though she was a poor cook and the Lindies were always grubby and noisy, was the right wife for Dad. He was a man who needed a congenial peaceful slob by his side, and he certainly had one.

Malcolm was at Tech, doing automotive engineering. He was rapt in anything on wheels, with a natural genius for engines. Not that it was apparent. He was a big boy, a bit of an Ocker, with a Viking moustache and beggar's clothes and a string of interchangeable girlfriends. But his fanaticism about the old Jowett Long Four was indicative enough. He would have garaged it in his bedroom had it fitted, and if Harry or Dad as much as breathed on it he went on like a nutcase.

Being in the used-car business himself, Dad sometimes came across prehistoric automobiles, some with chooks

72

nesting in the seat stuffing and possums holed up in the radiators. He took them home, and Malc and the current girlfriend then spent countless hours of hard labour on them, getting them roadworthy and selling them for large profits. The girlfriends all put up a good show of being besotted about old cars, even when they didn't know a spark plug from a piston. They had changed so often in the year Harry had been in Sydney that now he didn't even bother to learn their names. They came, they went, sometimes with fireworks and tears but mostly in an almost imperceptible fade-out as if they'd grown transparent. Malcolm was never crude or nasty to them. He just stopped noticing that they were around.

The current girl, however, was a real person. She was tall and as slim as a stick, with four ear-rings on her left ear. She always wore wrinkly pirate boots with shiny metal ornamented heels. Sometimes Malcolm chaffed her about them, and she took no notice at all. Harry rather liked that.

Laurel knew a great deal about vintage and veteran cars, because her old man owned two. He had the fabulous Opel-Darraoq Double Phaeton of 1905, with half-straight rear mudguards and a fold-up hood. And he had a Renault 45 from 1922. It had a long torpedo snout and a totally psycho radiator grille.

Malcolm preferred British cars, and it had always been understood that one day he would find just the wreck he wanted, and do it up like a jewel and drive it until one or the other of them died.

It was just like the discovery of America, or atomic fission, or something, thought Harry, the day Malcolm had towed home a Jowett tourer. Though when he learned that it had been bought from Amigo's Fair

Deals, the Best in Experienced Wheels, Dad breathed heavily. Amigo was a dicey character notorious for squeezing the golden juice from car-crazy European migrants.

Malcolm took a first-sight fancy to the Jowett, perhaps because it was a historic make often used for police cars in England, or because few such cars had been exported to Australia, or because of its long shapely chassis painted a pumpkin yellow which even now had a sort of rich gloss, discernible amongst all the dents and bashes and dulled pimply patches where some Goth had tried to get off the original enamel with a blow-lamp.

'You should have seen her when I found her in the lot,' said Malc, sounding as if he had a bad cold.

'A crying shame, an old beauty like that,' said Dad. He was not a car freak like Malc, but he was cluey. So he knew that although Mr Amigo had sold the Jowett to Malcolm as a genuine 1926 model, the presence of the detachable cylinder heads proved that, in fact, it belonged to 1929 or later. He offered to go back to Amigo and get Malc's money back, but Malcolm went himself more as a demo than an aggro, as he said.

Mr Amigo just laughed. 'Boy,' he said 'you bought a wreck, not a history book. I tell you what was told me. I'm no expert on them dinnysaws. As is, where is, that was our agreement, and for two twenny bucks you got yourself a real museum piece.'

Dad went on a bit about ethics, but Malcolm wasn't listening. From the beginning he was obsessed with the old yellow tourer. No more did he waste time restoring other old bombs. Whatever time was left over from his Tech course was spent with the Jowett. And usually Laurel, industrious, quiet and knowledgeable.

Near the front of the hairy house at Saltbox Point, the bit that sloped down to the Harbour through a wilderness of crepe myrtle and grape and choko vines, was an old boatshed that Malcolm had converted into a workshop. He was fanatic about his tools, too, and was capable of making all kinds of spare parts. In the vacation he had gone all the way to South Australia to examine the products of an eccentric firm manufacturing the waterproof fabric originally used for the folding hoods of such archaic vehicles as the Jowett.

Of course the old car wasn't finished yet by a long way, but her engine was good for short runs and she looked a dream.

Still, that didn't explain a rear-vision mirror which reflected a face that wasn't there. After his first shock, Harry began to feel scientific about it. He would have liked to tell someone, and once or twice he considered having a word with Peke, who was so non-silly. But how to put it?

'Well, Peke, it was a man's face, darkish hair, one of those old-fashioned felt hats with a dent in the crown. No beard or anything, but they didn't in those days, did they?'

Not for a moment had it entered Harry's head that the man was of this present time; he had the flattened look of people in old movies or photographs. That wasn't the disturbing thing, though. *That* was the look on the man's face. Never had Harry seen such half-demented rage except once on a wild tomcat two dogs had bailed up in a corner. Eyes bulging, lips stretched tight over teeth so that sunlight glittered on two gold fillings at one side of the mouth. These fillings made Harry all the surer that the man belonged to some past era, for surely dentists didn't put gold in people's teeth any more? It was just too gruesome.

What had made the man so angry, and with whom? Harry had seen some cannibal expressions on drivers in his day, but nothing like this. This man looked as if he wanted to murder someone.

The more Harry pondered about it, the more curious he became. He didn't want to see that face again, but conscientiously he felt it was his duty to do so. It was obvious that Malc didn't see it, nor Laurel. Besides, there was something else. Malcolm seemed to be different. First it was only towards Laurel. Malc was often snappish with her, sometimes even spiteful. Harry was regretful. At first he thought it was just time for Laurel to do the fade act. And yet Malc hadn't gone on like this with the other girlfriends. He was a roughie, but he was no creep.

Also he was curt and offhand with the Lindies, and once or twice Harry heard him say sneering things to Peke that he thought downright gross. It was queer. And another odd thing was that though for weeks and months no profane foot had been allowed to touch that sacred running board, now Malcolm was generous – even pressing – with his offer of rides. Quite often he jerked his head at Harry or Laurel and asked, 'Come for a spin round the block?'

Harry would climb into the back seat, his body moving nimbly and his spirit as reluctantly as honey straight out of the refrigerator. He had no fancy to see the face in the mirror again, because the thing was becoming clearer. Now he could see that the man wore a preposterous striped tie, hooped out and secured to his shirt by a gold tie-pin.

The time after that Harry observed that the tie-pin was shaped like a horse's head, with a red stone for an eye. Then he began to see the edge of a V-necked jumper in an ugly geometrical pattern. Casually he asked his father, 'Did you ever wear a V-neck jumper when you were a young guy, Dad?'

'Sure I did,' said Dad. 'With no sleeves and a zigzag pattern like a carpet. I must have looked a clown. Why, are they coming in again?'

'Thought I saw one on TV,' said Harry.

Malcolm was now so rapt in the car that he cut classes, something he'd never done before. Laurel was there only at weekends, for she was a full-time student. It was distasteful to Harry to see her handing spanners and screwdrivers and hardly being spoken to. He began to wish she'd belt Malcolm a good one over the head with one of her wrinkly boots and push off with dignity. But she didn't.

Peke looked a bit wan. She said it was the heat and the baby teething. And Harry's father sometimes looked a lot older and draggier, as though he were working too hard. There was just this little change in this and that, and Harry wasn't sure he wasn't imagining it. However, there was no doubt that the man in the mirror was becoming more distinct. Harry looked at the mirror as often as he could bear to, sometimes seeing an overtaking vehicle but more often the brown shelly eyes of the man, wide and fixed, looking hard to the touch, like the eyes of a giant insect. Worse than that, Harry was beginning to hear things. Once a child crying, soft and muffled and far away, and another time a woman saying something though what he could not distinguish. But she sounded distressed.

Harry had an unselfconscious respect for his intellectual powers, so not for a moment did he think that perhaps he had blown his mind. It was plain that there was something very wrong with the old yellow tourer. But what? And how to find out?

It was Saturday morning, the first of the summer holidays, as he stooged around in the sunlight, thinking hard, kicking things. He tried to punt a choko over the fence but it came asunder and stuck on the toe of his sneaker, green gunk and even worse brown gunk, with big gummy seeds in it. This made him so uncharacteristically tetchy that he was disturbed.

He knew very well that other people's soap operas upset him, put him out of sync with his temperament. And, after all, it was *his* temperament. He had learned to live with it and it was unlikely it would change much now. He resented the impingement of these other people's lives. Probably it could be said, and rightly, that whatever was happening had nothing to do with Harry Punch. But the kind of changes that were around were ugly. Harry had this unshakeable feeling that they were not only associated with the old yellow tourer; they were associated with the Dad-Peke-Lindies set up. And that Harry didn't want to see interfered with by anyone or anything, for it was so right and comfortable for them all.

Right then, what about the Jowett Long Four? A car didn't have an evil-tempered spook visible in its rear-vision mirror for nothing. It struck him then that he ought to wander along and see if Mr Amigo of Fair Deals could tell him anything of the vehicle's history. Mr Amigo had never seen him, so he would tell him he was doing a school project for next year on vintage cars, and had come directly to the expert. Harry's experience was that adults would believe any kid who came seeking help for a project, no matter how witless the subject.

Mr Amigo certainly had an immense stable of Experienced Wheels, from flossy little Toranas (only one old lady owner) to colossal Chryslers shaped like hearses. As Mr Amigo had just finished cheating a Turkish migrant with three hundred dollars and twelve words of English, he was jovial.

'What you want, champ?'

While Harry explained about the project Mr Amigo's eyes roved about the lot looking for customers like a wasp looking for jam. They were yellow stripey eyes, too, a long way in. He said brusquely, 'No time, kid. Take off.'

'I just want to ask a few questions, SIR,' appealed Harry nicely. 'About a couple of old models, say a Jowett Long Four?'

Instantly the man turned the stripy eyes on him. 'Hey, dint I see you riding round with the young flashy bought the old yella tourer?'

Harry's heart sank, but he said coolly, 'Yes, sir, that's why I chose that model for my project because I can take photos, and describe its engine and all. But I ought to know something of its history, who sold it to you and that kind of stuff.'

Mr Amigo went off like a grenade. His eyes retreated so far they vanished. He shouted, 'Hah! You think me a socker? You tell that flashy I got more nous in one hair in my ear than he has in his whole body. Ought to be ashamed, sending his kid brother along to snoop. Told him when he come before, as is, where is – that's our agreement.'

Harry could have kicked himself. Of course now he remembered that Malc, with Dad's urging, had returned to query the year of the Jowett's origin. Old Nousy-Ears was certainly on the ball. He said placatingly, 'Gee, no, Mr Amigo, my brother is rapt in the old car, he's not a bit dissatisfied with it. She's running like a river, you must have noticed that if you saw me in it. It's just my project, you see. I want to know about the car's history, whatever you can tell me, that's all.'

Mr Amigo cooled down somewhat and his eyes came back.

'What you think I am, an elephant? I sell thousands of cars, thousands. How I remember who sold me what? Get lost. Time means money to a man like me. Good day, champ!' he suddenly yelled at a man who was furtively poking around a Rover that looked as if it had been entirely reconstructed by a panel-beater. 'You know a classy job when you see one, champ, only one owner, what you got for a trade-in?'

Pensively Harry went away. He was briefly chagrined that he had been caught out, but this passed. How could he know that Mr Amigo had spotted him with Malcolm and Laurel in the car? That was just bad luck. The other thing was that he was fairly sure Mr Amigo did have a memory like an elephant. He was the kind of man who would have himself covered legally on every side. Probably had records of every vehicle that had ever passed through his used-car lot. Still, he wasn't going to tell. Because even with the abuse and the eyes falling backwards in the head and the lavender face and everything, Harry had observed that Mr Amigo had a . . . guilty? . . . no, uneasy look.

Altogether it was an uneasy day, hot and sulky, with

an oozing wind strong enough to stir up dust and grit but not to move the smog that hung over the city. Dad was going to some public-relations party and had put on a pimply blue dacron suit with foul buttons like bits of old dog's bones. At the lunch table Malcolm would not leave that suit alone, sniding away at it until at last Dad, who had been taking his remarks with less and less good humour, told him to shut his trap, and if he thought his own backside was any treat for sore eyes in those bagged-out football shorts he had another think coming. Then he said he had to get a wriggle on, no time for a cup of tea, and went, relieved to do so as Harry could well see.

Malcolm then fell into a morose silence, shovelling in salad, and sometimes shooting Peke a derisive half-grin because the food, as Harry had to admit, was pretty barbaric. Peke was the only person he knew who could limpen a fresh lettuce, and her sliced tomatoes were soggy red rings with nothing in the middle.

The bitter baby was bawling away in the pram on the verandah, and the Mindies were in fearful tempers because of heat rash. The twins glared as one child at Malcolm.

'Look, Mum, Malcie hasn't washed his hands. All gurky black grease under his fingernails, look Harry.'

'And in his mo, too,' said the third Lindy. 'We hate mos, don't we, Mum, urk, yuk, byah!'

'Shut your ugly little bug faces!' shouted Malcolm. With a pang of true sympathy Harry saw Peke looking thoughtfully at her three daughters as if they might really have a resemblance to bugs. She was a very fair-minded person.

The twins, however, did not care for the remark, and

the fatter one sank her tiny short teeth into Malcolm's hand. Malcolm swore and jumped up shaking his hand as if an alligator had almost taken it off. For a moment he wore such a ferocious grimace that Harry half-rose, thinking his brother was going to take a swipe at the child. The next moment, like magic, Malc's face smoothed out. It wasn't red any longer. He said with a laugh, 'Little beast, you ought to be behind bars. I say, Peke, let's take the kids out for a run, in the park down by the estuary bridge perhaps? Cool us all off. Time the old yellow tourer had a spin, anyway.'

The Mindies went into raptures, for they'd never been allowed near the tourer, let alone offered a ride in it. But the odd thing was that Peke became pale, nervously said perhaps not this time, for the baby was so tetchy with her new tooth, the older children should really have a nap, she herself had one of her sore throats coming on with the smog – the excuses were all so made up that once again Malcolm's disdainful sneer appeared, and his big smiling boy's mouth took on a looser, crueller look. Harry's skin began to prickle. Against his will he flicked a glance at Laurel to see if she had noticed too.

Then Laurel, who had said almost nothing during lunch, spoke in her slow, calm way. 'You're the one who needs the nap, Peke. Tell you what. Harry and I will go with Malc and look after the kids for a couple of hours.'

Harry was amazed to see Peke turn paler still. She cast at her children a look that was almost desperate, like that of a mother cat whose young kittens are being played with too long and too roughly. But she didn't know how to say no. And at the same time she could not bear to let her children go away from her. She didn't know why, Harry could see that, and all at once he became not only puzzled but very frightened as though Peke knew, or suspected, something dreadful. Or just felt it in her bones? Because she looked quite different, yellowish, with big staring eyes. Harry sat rigidly, his thoughts going no further because just then she said hurriedly to Malc, 'No, no, I'll come, it will be a break from the house, always cooler down by the water, the children can paddle.'

'Good,' smiled Malcolm, 'and Harry and Laurel will wash up while we're gone.'

'Come on,' said Laurel with a sharp tone Harry had never heard from her before. 'It would be no break for Peke to look after three children under five, not to mention the baby. Harry and I will come and give her a hand with them.'

'I don't recall inviting either you or Harry, Laurel,' said Malc, in a voice electric with fury.

In a moment there was as showy a row as Harry ever hoped not to see. Laurel threw everything at Malc, his selfishness, his childish obsession with the car, his pig's manners with the food, the mean way he had criticised his father's new horror suit when obviously the old man was so pleased with it. Now and then Peke, clutching excited and thrilled children to her, murmured, 'I don't really mind . . . some other time . . . all saying things we don't mean . . .'

No matter what Malcolm yelled, Laurel yelled him down. And every word she said, Harry thought, was right on. At last Malcolm was quiet. A funny smile, almost gloating, flickered over his face. He said ruefully, 'Of course you're right, love. I'm sorry, Peke, if I've been a pain in the neck. And poor old Dad! I was just putting him on but . . . okay, everyone, sorry, sorry, sorry. And you're invited to come for a run to the park in the Jowett, the whole lot of you.'

One of the Cindies threw her arms around his legs. 'You're a sweet kind Malcie and we love you and we won't never bite you again.'

'Of course you won't,' said Malcolm gently, ruffling up her reddish wisps of hair.

Harry got up, feeling uncertain on his legs, as if he'd been asleep and wasn't quite with it yet. Everything seemed a bit off key. The fight wasn't anything, everyone had fights, especially guys and their chicks. It wasn't poor old Peke being fraught, or the kids biting or bawling, because all those things happened every day, to some humans, anyway. There was just the weird sensation that things weren't quite square, the lines were off-level, they didn't meet in infinity and perhaps nothing did.

They piled into the Jowett. Like all tourers, it was a roomy car. Harry noticed Peke look around distractedly for seat belts and then sigh resignedly as she remembered that in such old cars such devices were not compulsory. Laurel sat in the front with one of the twins in her lap and a Lindy by her side. The little girls twined themselves around her like vines, and Harry, knowing how fantastically hot little children are, wondered how she could stand it. Malcolm, humming to himself, all the fuss forgotten, beamed around as he started the car. He was especially nice to Laurel, as though her blow-up had been something he'd been waiting for and was satisfied now that she'd done it.

Harry sat in the back seat with Peke, the other twin between them, and the baby, which had now been fed and was asleep, emitting the agreeable odour of warm puppy which Harry had noticed was common to healthy infants, lay on Peke's thin knees. A trickle of water ran down Peke's Indian cotton skirt, but she didn't seem to notice, so Harry ignored it. He supposed mothers could get used to anything.

In no way in the world was Harry happy. He was boiling hot, and he was scared. The only thing that was good was that he and Laurel were there with Peke and the Mindies. For in a freaky way he felt that Malc wanted only Peke and the kids in the car. While he was frazzling over this, Malcolm half-turned round and said almost dreamily to him, 'You've no place there.'

The Mindy lolling on Harry said at once, 'Harry's got plenty of room. Harry likes being squashed, don't you, lovely Harry?' But Harry instantly knew what Malcolm meant. He, Harry, wasn't in the cast, and neither was Laurel. He didn't know what that meant; he only knew that it was true, and urgent, and dreadful. He cast a look in the rear-vision mirror and there the man was, clear as day, the expression on his face like that of a wolverine. Mad. A demon's face. His teeth were bared, his dark, shelly-looking eyes unblinking. As Harry gasped at this horrific face, his heart whaling away against his ribs, the car filled with a dank, watery reek, and he began to hear swashy sounds, and the ever-increasing babble of human voices, almost within his range of hearing but not quite, except in patches, like a bad phone connection. There were children shrieking, and a woman saying, 'No, Murray . . . stop, Murray . . . didn't mean . . . the children . . . Murray . . . please.'

The whole thing was so dreadful that Harry's thoughts completely jumped the track. He just sat, aghast, not knowing what to do. The man in the mirror kept on laughing. The sun glittered on the red eye of his horse-head tie-pin, and his gold teeth and his glassy eyeballs. Now they had turned out of the streets Harry knew, and were sailing down a steep grade. The Jowett's cruising speed was about fifty-eight k.p.h. but Malcolm usually chugged along at a sedate thirty-two. Now the vehicle, gathering speed, raced down the narrow bendy road to the estuary. Harry saw the struts of the old wooden bridge appearing and vanishing as the trees whizzed past. Council was always threatening to knock it down, for motorists rarely used it now that the highway had been put through to the south. Demolish it and fill in the tail-end of the estuary and let's have more parkland, the Progress Association urged, but nothing had been done as yet.

Peke cried, 'You're going too fast, Malc!'

The baby awakened and screeched.

'Rot,' said Malcolm, grinning back at Peke, and his eyes were brown and shelly, looking as if they'd be hard to touch. 'She's got great brakes. I'll stop just when I please.'

Now the air inside the car had a quivering greasy look. Harry could hardly make out Peke's features as she shrank back in her corner, the back-seat twin having flung itself all over her like a child-shaped rug. The sounds had come back, louder, yet more confused, and these noises from nowhere were like an obbligato to the real sounds – Laurel shouting at Malc to stop, and the children howling, and the old car creaking and grinding as she had never done before. About the only clear thing in the whole scene was the man in the mirror, laughing without a sound.

The flame trees pressing close to the roadside flew

past like towers on fire, the car lurched through the park gates, people started up from the grass in fright or amazement, and a dog side-slipped the front wheels by centimetres. The bridge, picturesque, rickety-looking, was before them, spanning the sloshing rising tide. And Harry knew, as if he'd read it somewhere, what Malcolm intended to do.

He yelled to Laurel, 'Give me your boot!'

Without a question she whipped off her boot and thrust it at him, and without hesitation he leaned dangerously far out of the window and whacked the heavy heel with all his strength at the rear-vision mirror. As the glass smashed, Malcolm jammed on the brake, but too late.

The bridge railing splintered and gave way, the bonnet of the car hung partly over the drop, one wheel still spinning madly, and Malcolm himself was thrown against the steering wheel, his nose bleeding like a running tap. The Lindies were shrilling like sirens, the baby fountained milk all over Peke, and from every side people ran towards them.

Shakily Harry scrambled out. He wanted to help Peke but his legs would hardly bear him. He watched Laurel doing practical things, lifting out the children, mopping the blood from Malc, even speaking sensibly to the police when they and the ambulance arrived. Then she put an arm around Harry's shoulders as he clung to the shattered railing, and together they looked down into the deep swirling water. It was an ugly polluted greenish-brown.

Laurel said nothing but, 'Malcolm's all right, you know. Broken nose, I should think. Won't improve his beauty, though!'

It was generally believed that the brakes of the old car had failed. 'But they didn't, you know,' said Harry to his father. 'We have to find out where that car came from, whether it was ever in another accident.'

Because his father recognised Harry's good sense, he took him seriously when he told him what he had seen and heard.

'Police records,' he said.

But they could find no record of a car going over the side of the estuary bridge. However, the police sergeant suggested that they check the files of one of the big Sydney dailies. It was easy to find the report of a certain accident in the cross-index, and soon they were examining the file for November 1932.

There was a blurry picture of the Jowett upside down in the Clarence River, the spokes of the one visible wheel clogged with driftwood and rubbish.

'Nasty way to go,' said Dad, shuddering.

Murray Greenhill, his name had been, that original owner of the old yellow tourer. In 1932, for reasons of his own, he had crashed the car through the railings of a bridge and drowned his wife and himself and their four children. Witnesses at the inquest stated that he had been a surly, suspicious type of man, and his wife had seemed timid and unhappy. The verdict was that he had been of unsound mind.

'Wonder how the car got down here from the Clarence?' said Dad.

Harry thought of the Jowett in a shed or barn, covered in cobwebs as well as river mud. And then someone had restored it, got it back on the road, even had other accidents, until finally it had ended amongst Amigo's Experienced Wheels. It would have no more accidents.

Malcolm had agreed to have it towed away to be pulped.

Malcolm was home from hospital, cheerful and without worries, making unintelligible jokes about his bashed-in, bandaged nose.

'Damned if I can understand his snuffles,' said Dad, 'but Laurel seems to be able to translate. They're talking about going skiing next winter.'

Back home in Saltbox Point, Harry went off and had a punt at another choko. This time it sailed over the fence in a perfect arc. He decided not to think about what had happened any more.

GETTING THROUGH SUNDAY

RICH WAS ONE THING the Rich family was not. Still, its members got by.

The family consisted of Dad, Mum, Bud and Nathan, who was thirteen. They were on their way to a holiday in the Warrumbungle Mountains in north-west New South Wales, and Bud had been yammering at her parents for the best part of 500 kilometres.

Ten-year-old Bud didn't want a family holiday and was prepared to make a disaster of it. Fortunately Nathan had the ability to tune out and not hear the boring script that was now on its fiftieth rerun.

Mum said, 'You must try to understand, Bud.'

'Other people's families arrange things better,' said Bud in the sneering voice that always made Nathan want to murder her. 'They use their credit cards so their kids can have a really ripper time, skiing and that.'

Dad protested, 'I've told you and told you I won't do that. We're just keeping afloat as it is, don't you understand?'

Often Nathan saw a flare of resentment in Dad's eyes. Maybe grief, too, that he couldn't do what other fathers could. Then Nathan raged inside, and silently he shouted, 'You don't have to defend yourself! Why do you let her get away with it?'

Nathan had always thought of himself as the real child of the Rich family. The other one sort of attached itself when no one was looking and was cared for like a stray kitten. Bud had been a frail baby and Nathan supposed Mum had worried about her. He had never been jealous and indeed had liked Bud a lot until she was nine or so, when she turned into a piranha who seemed to think her sole function in life was to make it unbearable for others. This phenomenon was not unusual. Several of his friends had sisters or brothers equally foul, dedicated to tireless teasing or campaigns of spite that got the victim into hideous trouble.

He and his mates thought it was a kind of trend like the other that went along with it, the wimping of parents who let kids like Bud shove them around, all in the name of tolerance and love. It was a mystery.

However, Nathan had been on top of the Bud problem for six months now. It had taken nerve and willpower, but at last he had achieved it. She never got a rise out of him no matter what she did. He just behaved as though she were not there. Let her turn on a tantrum, let her take bright green poison in front of his very eyes, and Nathan would not even notice. He would step over her body and remain cool. But he still became upset inwardly when she behaved so badly to Mum and Dad. They didn't deserve it, unless wimps deserved all they received, which he sometimes believed.

Anyway, here they were, en route to a fabulous holiday and all of them as miserable as wet dogs.

'Wow!' exclaimed Dad. 'How's that for terrific?'

The back of his neck always turned pink when he was excited. Now it was beetroot red. He waved an arm out the car window.

The edge of the plain, blond with wheat and blooming sunflowers, bristled with the spikes and cupolas of the Warrumbungles. They were as blue as thundercloud.

'How did they get to be those weird shapes?' marvelled Mum.

'I want to go home!' grizzled Bud. 'At least when I'm home I can ring my friends.'

'Drop dead!' thought Nathan.

Mum said anxiously, 'Well, maybe you can ring

someone from Coonabarabran. How about Madalyn? That'd be all right, wouldn't it, Chris?'

Nathan could see it wasn't, country calls costing what they did. Still, Dad nodded, and Bud leaned contentedly back and closed her eyes, now and then snickering. Nathan knew she was working out what she would say to her friend Madalyn.

In the semi-silence Nathan began to feel cheerful. He pondered on the mountains. The Bungles, people around here called them, a jokey name. But they were not jokey mountains. They had a remote, alien look, as though they had nothing whatever to do with the golden plain surrounding them. Even on this sunny afternoon mist breathed stealthily out of their gullies, so that some of the vast stony wings and crumbled towers seemed to float on air, like a mirage. They were truly way out.

Dad had told Nathan the Warrumbungles hadn't been formed like ordinary mountains. They were the solidified cores of hundreds of prehistoric volcanoes. Imagine volcanoes just across the wheatfields there, howling and banging and whooshing! Nathan could visualise that hundred-million-year-old scene very well. It wasn't only scary, it was awesome, and made him feel as big as a pea.

He was quite relieved when he was jolted out of his reverie as they crossed the Castlereagh River at the old stock ford, and so drove into Coonabarabran.

It was a prosperous, wide-streeted town close to the foothills. Passers-by noticed the dust thick on the car, and gave the family a hospitable wave. Dad crawled out and rubbed his thighs; he was stiff and cramped after the two-day drive. He looked around with increasing cheerfulness, for he was a countryman at heart.

Bud glanced up and down the street, spied the post office and bolted.

'Hey, what about money for the call?' asked Mum. 'I'd better go too.'

'Bud's got her pocket money,' grunted Dad. 'Let her use that.'

Nathan was pleasantly surprised. They sat down at an open air cafe and ordered a mixed grill. While it was cooking Nathan wandered down the road. He liked the comfortable old town. It had a smell of sunburned dust and elderly stone buildings. Cedars grew in the main street and willows about the river.

He went into a shop where the shopkeeper was preparing to lock up for the night and bought a tourist information book for himself and T-shirts for the others. It took most of his allowance but he didn't mind. Mum's was red, with *Girl of the Golden West* on the front. Dad's was green with *I'm the Best, Wanna Argue?* Nathan did, in fact, think his Dad was the best. They had a top relationship. They liked the same things, soccer and fishing and video games and being left in peace.

He saw his mother go across the road to the post office, and come out with Bud. Bud was going on like a mad dog. Her yapping sounded up and down the street in the clear air of Coonabarabran. The post office doors closed behind them.

By the time he reached the table, where the mixed grill smoked on a huge platter, his father looked embarrassed and his Mum was about as annoyed as she ever got.

'They have to shut on time, Bud. Don't be so silly.'

'I only had time to ring Madalyn,' squalled Bud.

'Well, I guess that was all you had money for,' commented Dad, helping himself to salad.

A triumphant smile stole over Bud's face, and Nathan felt an anticipatory prickle run down his back.

'Oh, I asked Madalyn's mother if the call could be collect. She knows we're doing this trip el cheapo.'

Mum flushed. Dad slammed down his fork.

'Bud,' said Mum angrily. 'That's awful. I'm just so ashamed. Whatever will Madalyn's mother think?'

'Oh, she understood,' said Bud chirpily, picking up a sausage in her fingers. 'I told her this holiday was to let you and Dad work things out before you decide about splitting up.'

'That's family business!' said Dad hoarsely. His eyes almost sparked. His face was now dark red, so that Mum said hastily, 'Okay, leave it, leave it! I'll speak to Bud later. Eat up, Nathan, we have to get to the motel before dark.'

Nathan knew Mum was thinking of Dad's high blood pressure. He glared at Bud, but she was chewing away at the sausage, watching the birds homing in the high sunshine, an expression of such innocence on her face he could not for the life of him decide whether all her fiendishness was because she was only a kid, and maybe a dumb one at that. He even gave her the T-shirt. To his surprise she liked it. She put it on at once, saying yellow was her favourite colour and Madalyn's too. She tried to read the inscription upside down.

'I'm a little what? What's it say, Dad?'

Dad did not answer. He piled them all in the car, and drove off towards the Warrumbungles with noisy speed. Bud did not notice his fury.

'What is it, Nathan?'

'Yowie! Yowie!' growled Nathan.

'What's that?'

97

'Dunno,' said Nathan. 'Some extinct animal or other. Belt up, will you?'

Bud settled back and was as quiet as a mouse for the rest of the way. His father uttered a stifled sigh. Nathan could have sighed with him. Poor old guy, he thought, forty-three and already a big hole in his hair. Wife moaning around about leaving him, the factory on the verge of going bust, and a piranha for a daughter. But then, if Mum cleared out, maybe she'd take Bud. He didn't want to lose Mum, no way. But if Bud went too, it might be worth it. He would stay with Dad, no matter what.

Right there, Nathan stopped thinking. The whole thing embarrassed him a lot.

It was midsummer; the dark sifted down softly, the darkness in the humid gorges of the Warrumbungles rising to meet it. Already Nathan could smell eucalyptus leaves and moss and wet stones. Like his father, he was a countryman, even if he had been born in Sydney. He liked creeks and trees, and stuff like that.

They came at last to the lighted motel. The air had a true bush chill, and the woman who met them at the office door had rosy cheeks.

The motel accommodation was the kind Nathan liked – one large room with seven bunks, and a kitchen and bathroom off it. It was hospital clean, and equipped with everything, but it still had the nice homely air of a camp.

'A fishing camp?' wondered Dad aloud.

'Mostly trampers and rock climbers,' corrected the manager. 'But the Castlereagh runs at the bottom of the paddock out there. It's a baby, only about two metres wide, because it rises yonder in the Bungles. There's yabbies in it, if you kids want to fish tomorrow.'

Nathan saw a familiar look of contempt and insolence steal over Bud's face. He dreaded her saying something rude to this friendly lady. But the manager went on, 'Now, if you'll take my advice, you'll drop all your luggage, and drive into the reserve a kilometre or two and see the flannel flowers by moonlight. You mightn't see such a show again in a thousand years, the season has been so good. While you're gone I'll pop some milk and bread and few oddments into your fridge to start you off.'

She had hardly whisked out before Bud said, 'I'm not going. Who wants to see dumb old flannel flowers?'

'You're coming,' said Dad stubbornly. 'You can do what I want, for a change.'

'Oh, for goodness sake, Chris,' said Mum tetchily. 'She's tired. She can stay here.'

'She's coming!' Dad seized Bud by the back of the yellow T-shirt, and, just as fast, Mum smacked away his hand.

'Just leave her alone, will you?'

Nathan had a lightning glimpse of Bud's glance going from one to the other with a kind of greedy triumph. All at once he understood that a lot of his parents' disagreements had been over his sister, one way or another, and Bud knew it and was puffed up with power because of it.

Budpower, thought Nathan. And for a moment he really hated Bud.

This realisation was too much for Nathan. He wanted to get out of there. Bud also seemed to find the tenseness disturbing. She bawled.

'You're so cruel to me,' she hiccuped. 'Never do anything I want! Madalyn says. All the girls say. Ought to run away. King's Cross. A shelter for mistreated kids. Hate everyone.'

In the end the girl and her mother stayed behind, and Nathan and Dad drove off to the national park. The car was full of uneasiness and it didn't all originate with Dad. Nathan was miserable, not knowing whether he should say something or not. At his age so many things he said got up people's noses, even though his intentions were of the best.

So he remained silent. Thoughts raced around in his head, shook themselves to pieces, returned again and again.

He understood Dad a little. Maybe even a lot. Of course Dad didn't really want Bud to come and see the flannel flowers. What he wanted was for Mum to come. But if Bud stayed back at the motel Mum would, too, and Dad was as badly off as ever, missing Mum's participation in a scene he wanted to see and thought would be special. And Bud had frustrated him, as easily as falling off a log.

Nathan couldn't see what he could do about it, so he tried to think about something else.

'Oh, mate!' breathed Dad suddenly. 'Will you look at *that*!'

He drove on to the verge and turned off the ignition. They got out into the cold moonlight, though it wasn't as much moonlight as an ethereal radiance drifting down from nowhere. Probably the moon was never seen at all in this precipitous glen, with the black crags and steeples of the Bungles pressing in all around. Only its light was present, showing the striped silver trunks of the beech trees, the chaos of tumbled rocks, the snow on the steep slopes.

Except that it wasn't snow, but flannel flowers, eddies and lagoons and rivers of them, luminously white, growing in every crevice, every pinch of soil, from the road's edge to the heights where the dusk took over.

Nathan and Dad walked slowly down the road, and everywhere the flowers grew in millions and billions. Dad gazed and gazed, his mouth open. He muttered things like, 'I never dreamed . . .' and 'A man might go his whole life without seeing something like this' and 'I mean, it really *is* like a snowfall.'

He was rapt. Nathan, who could take flowers or leave them, made what he hoped were agreeable noises. Certainly, it was pretty amazing, all these daisy things blooming at one time, some freak of rain or heat, Nathan guessed, but it wasn't a mega deal. However, plainly Dad felt differently. He was knocked out. Nathan was quite stunned to discover the old man felt like this. He'd never shown a sign of it before. It was creepy how grown-ups could conceal the way they really were, just as if they had invisible lives of their own. Unfair from the kids' point of view, and a bit sad, too.

'Out of this world,' said Dad at last, after they'd walked about a kilometre and the flowers showed no sign of petering out, though Dad did. 'Makes a lot of things worthwhile.'

Nathan remained silent, strolling along, feeling companionable and tolerant. The old man seemed to be in a waking dream, so much so that when Nathan spotted the glisten of big eyes as a kangaroo bounded between the fallen rocks, he didn't even mention it, for fear of bringing his father back to earth.

About the only thing Dad said was, 'I've always wanted to visit the Warrumbungles. Ever since I was a youngster. I saw a picture in a book, and they kind of caught my fancy. I'd like to see all I can while I'm here. Get up high and see all those queer-shaped peaks and bluffs. They look as if they belong in another world. I like that.'

Nathan was also surprised to know his Dad ever imagined other worlds. He had believed he mostly thought about the factory. But he was pleased to discover this new thing.

When they returned home Dad parked the car under a big willow. They could see a sheeny streak that was the infant Castlereagh, and hear its faint burble.

'We're going to have a top time,' said Dad cheerfully as they entered their motel room.

Mum was asleep, with a magazine in her hand and her glasses dropping off her nose. Bud was reading. She didn't even look up. So Nathan and Dad said nothing about the flannel flowers.

They had their showers, and went to bed, and no sooner was the light out than Bud started scratching the wall. Nathan could imagine that small sunburned hand gently scraping away at the bare wood, not loudly, just enough to keep people awake and maddened.

'Oh, God!' groaned Dad. 'Cut that out, will you, Bud?'

'I'm not doing anything,' said Bud crossly, 'and what's more you woke me up.'

Dad grunted. Nathan lay there in the country silence, absolutely nothing to be heard except a little wind cheeping somewhere. And of course Bud scratching the wall. Nathan knew she could keep it up for hours if need be, just as she could keep up kicking his chair at dinner.

He was determined not to show he noticed. That was all she wanted – to have someone lose his cool and yell at her. Would Dad do it? Nathan imagined him lying there with his teeth on edge just as he himself was, tired out from the long drive, snatched from his flannel-flower dream, worried about all kinds of things.

Scratch, scratch.

'Shut up!' yelled Dad suddenly.

Mum awakened with a start. 'What's all the row? What's the matter?'

'They're blaming me again, Mum,' wailed Bud. 'They won't let me go to sleep!'

Mum thumped out of bed and turned on the light. She was red-faced and furious. Bud, who could turn on tears like a tap, began to cry. Mum accused Dad, 'Can't we have any peace? What's she supposed to have done?'

In a moment the parents were firing cruel words at each other. Nathan rose as calmly as he could and said politely, 'Can I have the car keys, Dad?' It was a moment or two before his father paid any attention.

'What d'you want them for?'

'I'm going to sleep in the car.'

'Half your luck. They're on the table.'

As he slid the bolt on the door, Nathan saw his mother raise her hands despairingly. She said in her ordinary, warm voice, 'If we're like this Friday night how will we get through Sunday?'

It was the family's bad luck that Sundays were always the pits in their household. Dad was tired and edgy, Mum worried or bored or something, and Bud at her ingenious worst. Fortunately Madalyn's people were wealthy and sometimes they took Bud out on their luxury boat. Not nearly often enough however. Even then, with Bud out of the house, things were not great, with Mum and Dad fretfully sniping at him and each other. Nathan would have wiped Sundays out of the week if it had been possible.

He crunched over the wet grass to the car. The seat was a bit short for sleeping, but he was dead tired, and the fresh air had bowled him over. He was aware of the Castlereagh muttering, a night bird hoo-hooing, and somewhere far away a rooster going mad with the moonlight and blasting out a dawn cry. He had a grand sleep, all folded up like a safety pin and not dreaming of anything. Then suddenly, click, just like that, he opened his eyes and was wide awake.

Everything was black as black velvet. The car was freezing, even though he was warm under the blanket, for he'd left one of the front windows open a few centi- metres. He lay there wondering what had awakened him. Then he heard something walking on the roof of the car.

He snuggled down, grinning. It was a possum, maybe even a koala. But, as he listened, he became aware that the sounds were not those of an animal. They were not footsteps, or claws scrabbling, or a little scamper and a thump. They were more like . . .

'Oh, God,' breathed Nathan, swallowing hard. *Slithering*!

The next moment sanity returned. Snakes didn't come out at night. But suppose one had dropped by accident out of the willow tree, a tree snake? And was slithering along the car roof, ready to creep in through the open window? Nathan wasn't sure about tree snakes.

He sat up and pushed the blanket aside, ready to

thrust open the rear door and run if necessary. The sounds continued.

Nathan strained his ears in the blind darkness. He felt very nervous, just on the verge of being scared. Up and down, up and down, stealthy eerie sounds. *Patting* sounds. Small gentle taps. Just as if something was feeling along the car roof. Feeling for what? And why? Then, all at once the sounds stopped. The car lurched violently as if an elephant had given it a careless push. The bonnet, which was a little loose, rattled loudly.

Nathan was almost thrown out of the seat. Dumb with fright, he stared out of the window, but could not see anything. All was black as pitch.

Should he run for the motel?

No. He thought of all the fuss. Mum having a fit. Bud jeering. And besides, whatever it was – it might still be out there. He lay down again feeling shaky. Was it a cow? Oh, yes, he could just imagine a cow rearing up and tapping the top of a parked car! Anyway, cows didn't wander around at night. Well, what was it, then?

Unexpectedly, he fell asleep, to awaken hours later to find Dad at the window, carrying a cup of tea.

'Sleep well?' asked Dad.

Only a split second elapsed before Nathan replied, 'Great.'

When he left the car, he examined the roof, hoping to see small muddy paw prints there, but there was nothing but heavy dew. He began seriously to doubt himself. Had he really been awake or dreaming? By the time he got to the motel he wasn't sure at all. Anyway, it wasn't something he wanted to talk about.

Mum turned on a fabulous breakfast, hamburgers

and chips and tomatoes. Whenever Mum cooked that kind of breakfast, she was feeling guilty or conscientious. Nathan knew this by experience. He looked at her closely, and sure enough her eyes were red as though she'd had a rotten night. Dad defiantly shovelled a lot of salt on his plate and she didn't say a word. He wasn't supposed to have it because of his blood pressure.

Bud did her usual thing of turning over the food with her fork, poking at it, her expression one of amazement that anyone should actually expect her to eat this garbage.

'Eat it or put it away, Bud,' said Mum shortly. Bud shrugged, poked a bit more, and then, as no one watched her, began to eat.

They tidied up a little and then Dad said, 'Wear your hats and take the insect repellant. I'll drive you up to the rangers' information centre, and then you're on your own.'

'Where are you and Mum going?' asked Bud, almost in alarm.

'We've got things to talk about, so we're going to explore by ourselves.'

'We'll get lost!' objected Bud.

'No, we won't,' said Nathan. 'There are all kinds of guided walks leaving from the rangers' centre. I read about it in the brochure. And we can get maps and posters there too. Come on, we might meet some other kids. Not to mention native animals.'

Bud brightened. One good thing Nathan had to say about his sister, she liked animals. Probably all she did like except her friend, the nerd Madalyn. On the way into the National Park an emu strode across the road. Several times they saw groups of large grey kangaroos

106

goofing off in the shade, and once a frogmouth owl, fast asleep on a branch, and looking like a little branch itself.

Dad made inquiries at the centre about walks suitable for kids. Bud made no protest as he attached them to a party going off under the care of a volunteer guide.

'Meet us here at one o'clock,' said Mum, 'and we'll have a nice lunch in Coonabarabran.'

Nathan looked back as his parents turned off along one of the many bush tracks. He heard his mother laughing as she crossed the stepping stones across the shallow creek, and thought how great it'd be if they went back again to being sensible. He didn't know what their problem was.

What was the matter with the life they had? It wasn't terrific but it was all right. He looked around for Bud and saw she had joined a party of Japanese high-school students. Bud out in the world was not recognisable as Bud in the heart of the family. The pale, stick-legged sulky girl became a lively friendly kid. As Nathan watched her giggling and jumping around with the Japanese youngsters, he had an eerie feeling that he'd imagined all her awfulness at home.

'See!' A large hand fell on his shoulder. A huge, straw-haired boy, taller and broader than Nathan's father but undeniably a boy, pointed above them. Striped in yellow-grey, its agile feet grasping the bark like splayed hands, the creature on the tree-trunk turned its wise old-man's eyes upon them. It was as still as stone.

'It's a goanna!' said Nathan.

'No, no,' said the huge boy, hastily turning the pages of a pocketbook. 'It is a lace monitor. We are fortunate to see it. It is, I think, two metres long, like myself.'

'*We* call them goannas,' said Nathan.

'Ah. Common name,' said the boy, fetching out a ballpoint and scribbling the word in the book's margin. He held out his hand. 'I am Fred. From Sweden. You?'

They stayed together all morning. Fred and Nathan got on like a house afire. Fred was a rock climber. His fair face was sunburned to a scarlet which matched his shirt, and his eyes shone with the fever of obsession. He could not, on this trip, climb the more precipitous mountains.

'But I shall come back with a group, three years from now, and we shall climb the most dangerous. This week I am by myself and only play.'

Fred had come to the district primarily to visit the Siding Spring Observatory. He was astonished to discover Nathan had not heard of it.

'But it has some of the most advanced telescopes below the Equator. Wonderful, wonderful! No, you must see it, my friend.'

Before the boys parted they had talked about most of the things that interested them. Fred even had older and younger sisters who monstered him. Nathan thought that uncanny, but somehow comforting.

Fred laughed. 'Ah, some day someone will marry them. Anyway, I go to Stockholm to University next year. Science I study.'

After a few joking words, Fred shook hands with a giant's grip and plunged away through the scrub. Presently Nathan spied him scrambling up a steep slab towards a dome like a bombed castle. It rose from a jumble of shattered rock, over which the heat shimmered. Fred appeared and vanished, a small red spider on that wasteland.

'I should have given him my hat,' thought Nathan.

Somehow he had lost the walking party, so he meandered back along the track towards the information centre. He was astonishingly happy.

Mum and Dad and Bud were drinking Coke under a tree. They seemed relaxed and friendly, even though Mum put on her usual 'Where've you been, I've been worried out of my wits' performance.

'I met Fred,' explained Nathan. 'From Sweden. Rock climber.'

'Good bloke?' asked Dad.

'Guess so,' said Nathan. Mum went on a bit about his failure to get Fred's surname and address.

'You could have been penfriends,' she lamented. Dad winked at Nathan. He knew what Mum didn't, that the experience of meeting Fred was enough, part of the day, part of his memories of the Warrumbungles, like the goanna and the Japanese students.

Bud had the names and addresses of several of the Japanese kids. Over lunch, she talked about them intermittently, and then ran out of steam and became grumpy.

'I want to ring Madalyn,' she demanded.

'You are not going to ring Madalyn,' declared her mother. 'Not until I have a chance to apologise to her mother for your impertinence.'

Bud sulked, silent and glowering, refusing to join in the conversation . . . The rest of them had ice creams, but she wouldn't. She watched every mouthful Nathan took, a trick that brought him out in goose pimples, but he did not lose his composure for an instant.

'Oh, Bud, do stop it!' pleaded Mum.

Nathan was sorry that his parents didn't realise that the best way to treat his sister was to pretend she wasn't there. But he didn't suppose they could be told. Bud sulked for a while and then she began to make the weird clicking sound behind her nose that only she could make, as far as Nathan knew. Mum shifted nervously on her chair and Dad's neck flushed. Neither of them knew whether their daughter was afflicted with some hindrance in her breathing that she couldn't help. Doctors said not, but the parents were more inclined to believe Bud. Nathan, however, knew that she did it deliberately with the sole aim of driving other people off the planet.

He said quickly, 'It'd be keen if we could see Siding Spring Observatory.'

His father hadn't heard of it either, but his eyes lighted with enthusiasm. Thanks to Fred, Nathan was able to pass on a little information, so that the old man was all for going there at once. Bud said she'd rather die.

'All right!' said Mum resignedly. 'You and I will stay in Coonabarabran and play tennis.'

In the end that's what Bud and Mum did. Nathan and Dad drove off to view the huge pale domes set down amongst the Warrumbungles like a Martian colony. Nathan went out of his mind about that observatory. He knew immediately he wanted to be an astronomer. It was the most exciting thought he had ever had, a revolutionary thought.

Knowing what he wanted to do in life made Nathan feel very strong, even very safe. His private joy lasted through all the drag of picking up Mum and Bud and returning to the motel, even having dinner, which wasn't too terrific, either. He heard Bud's complaints only as a distant whine.

Getting into his bunk, he drifted into a daydream

which soon became a true dream in which he went to Stockholm and worked with Fred. They discovered a new galaxy together – the Fred-Rich Galaxy, it was called.

For Sunday Dad had planned a day-long bushwalk and a picnic in one of the shelter huts built for benighted rock climbers.

'It'll be the high point of our visit, an expedition we'll always remember,' he said enthusiastically. 'And high country too. We'll be able to see the Warrumbungles for a hundred kilometres.'

Nathan thought that probably Dad wanted to write his name and the date in some unobtrusive place on the wall of that hut, and why not? Nathan determined to write his, too.

Mum packed a super picnic. She even got up early to bake an egg and bacon pie, the family's special favourite.

'We absolutely must leave before the day gets hot,' she fretted, and went to bang on the bathroom door yet again. 'Bud, do hurry.'

'Only be a minute,' replied a muffled voice. Nathan could just imagine her sitting on the toilet seat grinning.

Nathan gave his father an I-told-you-so look. Dad's neck was already red. Bud had set herself against the expedition the night before. She didn't mind hiking with other kids but she wasn't going to drag around with her boring family for anyone. She'd stay at the motel and read. Dad had shut her up irritably.

Over breakfast she brought her objections up once more. This time Mum flared up.

'You're not staying here the whole day by yourself,' she said. 'Dad's gone to a lot of trouble to make this a family holiday, and it might be the last one we have, even if you don't realise it.'

Her lip trembled and she turned quickly away.

'Suits me,' said Bud nastily, scooting into the bathroom. Nathan saw at once that could well be a mistake for them all but how can you keep anyone out of the bathroom?

Nathan amused himself during the long wait by studying the route of their walk. Naturally the map of the national park had nothing on it but mountains with beautiful unreal names like Bress and Belougery, Bedarra and Febar. Also marked were camping sites and many creeks and their tributaries. It was satisfying to Nathan to think of all that great space without junk like airports and opera houses spoiling it.

By the time Bud emerged from the bathroom the sky was bleached with heat and Dad was speechless. He slammed out to the car, which he had already loaded, and sat there glowering.

They drove into the reserve as far as Camp Pincham and took to the bush.

'She'll be all right once we start walking,' Mum murmured to Dad.

'Want to bet?' thought Nathan, slipping into his pack.

Some great ideas are doomed from the start, and the family expedition was like that. The day was so hot the air quivered. The creeks were low and soupy; no native animals were to be seen. Nathan knew they would all be resting in the shade, the intelligent thing to do. But the Riches ploughed on in glum silence. They saw no other hikers or climbers; nothing moved but spiralling hosts of speedy orange butterflies. Bud stumped along at the tail of the party, not looking at anything, grunting when spoken to. She was like a black cloud on legs. Slowly Nathan felt his good spirits sinking and dying.

'For heaven's sake try to enjoy yourself, Bud!' Mum burst out at last. Bud just gave her a hostile look.

'I'm hot,' she grumbled.

'Who stayed in the bathroom three-quarters of an hour and made us late?' demanded Dad. 'We could have been there by now, and in the cool, too.'

'Where's *there*?' said Bud.

'You'll see,' Dad grunted.

The track crossed and recrossed Spirey Creek. The butterflies had gone. Their place was taken by maddening bushflies. Lustreless leaves hung vertically; wilted nettles and thistles lined the way. Now and then the path was joined by others, marked Fan's Horizon, Macha Tor, Bedarra Bluff.

The silence of the party was complete. Nathan thought it was amazing how one sourpuss could cast a gloom over other people. Of course, that was what Bud wanted, but how did it happen? It beat him. He was relieved when they came at last to a sign saying Gould's Circuit.

'The map shows some good lookouts along this track,' said Dad. He took off his hat and flapped at his face with it. He looked as if he had been boiled. 'When we've had a rest at one of them we'll go on to Balor Hut. There's a water tank there, too. It's only another kilometre or so.'

Nathan saw Mum choking back a groan. She had troublesome feet, and he supposed they were hurting. She whispered, 'Dad's overdoing it. He'll get sick.'

'He's waited a long time to do this. His whole life,' said Nathan.

'How do you know?'

'Told me,' mumbled Nathan. He realised that Mum wanted Dad to have told her, too. But that was not his business. He leaped ahead of her and reached the look-out only a step or two behind his father.

Nathan wasn't great on scenery. He liked bits of it best. A loop of river, or an angophora with its roots coiled around sandstone outcrops like powerful pink snakes. Or just a dusty road standing on end up a hillside. So it was as if the strange Warrumbungle landscape lunged at him from every direction, olive green and bronze and a hundred blues, beautiful and majestic but frightening too. Nathan felt himself the size of a ladybird, clinging to a rock, liable to be blown off any moment. He might have felt better if the mountains had been the ordinary kind, pyramids rising from the trees in an orderly way. Or rounded and sort of comfortable. Although no wind stirred the forest, out of its depths rose an oceanic sigh of captured air.

'I'm frightened,' said Bud, and began to cry.

'I've got a blister,' she sobbed, 'and I feel sick in the stomach and I want to go home.'

'Oh, Chris,' said Mum, distressed.

Bud certainly looked sickish. Her face was white and sweaty, with bits of leaf and yellow dirt stuck here and there. She thrust her head between her knees and said in a muffled voice, 'I don't like it up here, I'm scared.'

'Scared of what?' asked Dad gently.

'Scared of falling off!' sobbed Bud.

As this was something like the feeling Nathan had, though not so dramatically, he realised Bud was not pretending in order to be difficult. He glanced at his father. Dad's face was pale, too. More than that, he

114

looked beaten. He realised with a pang, a real ache, that the old man had set his heart on getting to the high shelter hut, to sit there looking out over the castles and spires of the mountains, maybe feeling that for once he'd done something rare and wonderful.

'I wanted to see everything,' said Dad forlornly like a kid.

'I'll take her back to the car, Chris,' said Mum then. 'You go on with Nathan and join us back at the camp after you've climbed to Balor Hut.'

'No!' blurted Nathan. 'I'll do it.' The second the words were out of his mouth he could have kicked himself. But they were said, and he followed them by a sullen mumble. 'Give me the car keys, Dad. And we'd better take something to eat and drink.'

'But do you really want . . .' began his mother.

'Yeah, yeah,' said Nathan impatiently, almost angrily. 'I've had enough for today. Right?'

On the steep downward track Bud began to perk up. Nathan mooched along, scowling. Naturally she wouldn't walk with him, but either lagged behind or galloped ahead of him, not speaking, not answering his shouts when she got out of sight. Not that he wanted to see the brat, but he felt responsible.

Once, however, she trotted back and said, 'I feel better now.'

When he didn't answer, she added, 'Why'd you say you'd come with me?' Nathan did not reply, and she added almost shyly, 'It's because you knew Mum wanted to go with Dad, isn't it?'

Luckily Nathan did not look at her in surprise, but kept staring ahead. Still, he was amazed, shocked almost, to find out Bud knew anything about the way their parents felt. It was like finding out the cat could play the piano.

'You don't believe Mum will leave Dad, do you?' she asked at last. Her voice sounded queer.

'Why don't you ask Madalyn's old lady?' he barked. 'She seems to have heard all about it from you, blabbermouth.'

He saw then that her eyes were full of tears. She spat a bitter word at him and raced off down the path. In a moment she was out of sight around the bend. When he reached the turn, she was nowhere to be seen. Nathan snorted. *He* had the car keys. He had nothing to fret about.

But he had forgotten the branch tracks. Would she remember that the right track back to Camp Pincham curved back and forth across Spirey Creek? She'd paid no attention to anything on the way up. He stood doubtfully at the first conjunction of paths that occurred below the Gould's Circuit notice.

'Bud!' he called. No reply. A troop of wallabies hopped slowly across the track, surveying him mildly.

'Bud!' he shouted. 'I can see some wallabies!'

He knew wallabies would bring her out of hiding, if hiding she was. But there was no sound. Nathan cursed. He got out his map to see where the tracks led. One went towards West Spirey Creek and the other to Bedarra Bluff. He ran a few hundred metres down the creek path, calling her name. He knew perfectly well what would happen. She'd lose herself in the bush through sheer devilment and he'd cop the blame. He returned to the signpost, and almost immediately he caught a flash of yellow halfway down the Bedarra Bluff track. The little fiend *was* hiding. She'd let him hunt for

116

her, go out of his mind, maybe get lost himself. Mum would go crazy, Dad would have a stroke, but did she think of that? He'd kill her.

But he'd give her a fright before he did. He went silently along the track. She crouched amongst the bushes, whining. Truly whining, like an unhappy animal. Nathan said, 'Hey, what's up?'

'Go away!' she shrieked. Her face was dirtier than ever, blubbered with tears. There was a bloody scrape on a knee.

'Did you fall over?'

'Go away, I said!' she yelled. 'You don't care about me, or anything. Mum going away, Dad . . .'

She sprang up and blundered away into the scrub. In a moment the bushes had swallowed her.

'Don't do that, Bud, you'll get lost! Come back here, you idiot.'

He barged after her. There was nothing else to do, the terrain was so rough, boulders poking through prickly undergrowth, sudden drops and crevices, slithery slides of soil so dry it had turned into beads and pills as hard as cement. He saw her slip, go rocketing down the slope, catching bushes and small trees, losing her grip, slipping, sliding, skidding on lichened rocks. Oh, God, he thought, if she breaks her leg, how will I be able to carry her up the slope? If she breaks her neck, what'll I tell Mum?

She stopped at last, against a fallen tree, her skinny chest heaving, scratches and grazes all over her. But she was all right. She looked up and scowled.

'What are you following me for?'

'To get you back to the track, dumbo.'

'I'll get back there myself.'

117

'Have you hurt yourself? Aw, come on, Bud, have a bit of brain, will you?'

'Piss off!'

He felt like doing just that. Ungrateful, unreasonable, mean, she sat there, dirty bloodstained legs stuck out, staring at the ground, licking a scratched hand and spitting out whatever she got from it. He knew how she felt; she'd made a fool of herself and wasn't going to admit it. Running away like that!

'You could have broken your neck, you knucklehead!'

'Fat lot you'd care.'

'I'm going,' said Nathan, turning to the grim, almost vertical slope. He knew that Bud, left to herself, not watched, would follow him at a distance. He made himself climb thirty or forty metres before he glanced behind him. He saw Bud picking her way along at the bottom of the slope, climbing over fallen rocks, blindly clawing at the dense, interlocked scrub.

'Bud!' he yelled in horror. 'That's not the way, Bud!'

He tumbled to the bottom again, and followed her.

His legs ached, there was a sharp pain in his side, and his arms bled from a dozen grazes. He'd never seen such fiercely hostile country in his life; he hadn't even imagined it. You couldn't do a damned thing with it except leave it to itself.

Suddenly he spotted Bud. Exhausted, she sprawled amongst the rocks, panting and sobbing, frightened beyond bearing.

'Bud, be sensible. Come on.'

He must have startled her, for she jumped up, took a step backward and vanished into the greenery. He heard a fading cry as she fell.

After a stupefied moment or two Nathan was able to move. He did not know whether she had fallen down a crevice or over a cliff, but it would not help if he did the same thing. He wriggled forward on his stomach, and came to an abrupt drop, curtained with flowering bushes. He parted them, craning over the edge, and saw far below Bud's yellow T-shirt.

He called fearfully, and then desperately, but she did not move. Nathan took off his pack, which all this time he had been wearing, and looked for a way down. He really did not feel much, just the knowledge that he had to get to Bud. He clambered down over the hooped roots of a dead tree. A cavernous green valley lay beneath; Bud lay on a ledge level with the tops of enormous trees. The cliff bulged; hand holds that he thought were rock proved themselves to be hard clay that broke away under his clutching fingers. He wriggled past a projection to find air on the other side and no way to get back. But two metres below him was the plain mark of Bud's slide down an inclined rockface. He let himself go and landed and skidded as she must have done. The breath was knocked out of him; he lay there whooping, knowing that within a few centimetres of his head was space.

'That's what happened to me, too,' Bud said. He inched back towards the cliff face, still whooping.

'I could murder you!' he rasped.

They crouched there in silence. A vast sigh of wind or water rose from the valley below. It was so deep the trees looked like moss or curled green hair. It was half a kilometre across. Cloud shadows swam swiftly over the mossy forest, darkened for a split second the treetops before them.

'I'm hungry,' said Bud. 'Thirsty, too. Where's your pack?'

Nathan jerked his head towards the top of the cliff behind them.

'Oh, clever!' said Bud.

He let her have it then, all the suppressed rage of more than a year. Her selfishness, her attention-getting tricks, her meanness towards other people, even good people like Mum and Dad, her skinny legs and birdy nose, her bloody-minded stupidity in running pellmell through unknown bushland. He didn't leave out a thing.

Bud sat sulkily staring at her feet. Once or twice something like a grin flitted across her face. At the time, Nathan was too churned up to notice. By now he had realised that the rockface behind them was unclimbable without aid, and the trees rising from the valley were too far away to jump into.

'Otherwise I could climb down. Get help.'

She didn't say anything. A long silence lay between them, then she whispered, 'We'll have to stay here forever and starve to death.'

'Right,' he said bitterly, wanting to scare her.

The ledge was fairly wide, at least a metre and a half. In one place there was a rain puddle.

'You'd better have a drink, if you're thirsty,' Nathan said gruffly.

She lapped up a little from her hands. So did Nathan. The water tasted strange. Probably it had picked up minerals from the rock. But after that drink he felt better.

'I wonder what they'll think,' said Bud. 'I mean, when they get back to the car.'

'They won't even be able to get into the car,' said Nathan. 'I've got the keys.'

'Someone might be at the camp though. To fetch the ranger or the police,' said Bud.

Nathan looked at his watch. He figured that he had left his parents at Gould's Circuit at nearly midday. They might get back to Camp Pincham at four or five and give the alarm. Dad was sensible. He'd work that out on the way back to the camp Bud and he might have taken the wrong turning.

'There are helicopters,' he said reluctantly at last. 'And spotter planes. People must occasionally get lost around here. Bushwalkers, and climbers, and people like that.'

He really didn't want to help Bud feel better. The whole thing was her silly fault and she ought to suffer. A bit, anyway.

'If they ever find us,' said Bud in a mourning voice. 'This is such a wilderness of a place.'

'Well, even if we do have to spend the night here it won't kill us,' snapped Nathan, already sick of Bud's gloom.

Bud got up and wandered along the ledge. It canted downwards under an overhang. Nathan wanted to tell her to be careful, but he thought she would be, anyway. Still, he kept an eye on her.

He saw her duck under the overhang. After a little while there was a squawk, and Bud came running along the ledge.

'You'll never guess! There's . . . there's bones!'

Nathan loathed any variety of insides, and he wasn't big on bones, either. So he gave Bud a look of distaste

and said, 'I suppose a kangaroo has fallen over
sometime.'

'No, no,' cried Bud, excitedly. 'Come and look!'

Nathan went. The overhang sheltered not only the
ledge but a long shallow hollow in the cliff face. Into this
cavity, some time before, something had dragged itself
to die. The bones were dry and yellowish, not disagreeable at all. Both leg bones were shattered, one across the
thigh, and the other below the knee. But still, the skeleton had kept together. Birds of prey or goannas had not
pulled it apart.

Nathan stared at it, dumb with shock. He couldn't
believe what he saw. He couldn't even believe the
thought – realisation, whatever it was – that scudded
across his mind. At last he blurted: 'It must be a horse.'

'Are you bananas?' cried Bud indignantly. 'It's a
human!'

Nathan wanted to get away from there, and he did.
He went quickly back along the ledge and sat down.
Bud followed him.

'Why is it so big?' she asked.

'I don't know,' snapped Nathan. He felt trembly,
really shaken. But Bud wasn't. She hurried back to the
overhang and squatted at the feet of the skeleton.

'Please excuse me,' she said. The bones were lying
almost straight, so Bud carefully walked, heel to toe, the
full length. She went back to Nathan, who had his head
down on his knees, feeling he had had enough of this
frightful Sunday. He didn't want any more of anything.
But at the same time he couldn't keep his mind off those
bones, those yellow bones.

'It's nearly two-and-a-half metres long,' announced
Bud.

'How do you know?'

'Measured it.'

Nathan sneered. 'What with, smarty?'

'My sneakers. They're 19.32 cm long. So . . .'

Nathan groaned. 'Oh, shut up. Anyway, no human is that tall.'

'This one is,' said Bud. 'And what's more it's a woman and she has a little kid in her arms. And the kid's big too.'

Nathan went and looked. There was a tangle of smaller bones inside the crossed arms. The bigger skull had dark coarse hair on its crown, and the smaller one a fleece of lighter hair.

'She fell over the cliff by accident, like I did,' said Bud, 'and broke her legs. The baby died of starvation.'

Amongst the ribs lay a bag of possum skin. Bud picked it up.

'Oh, yuk!'

'She won't mind,' said Bud. 'I bet she carried her treasures in it.'

The possum skin was not stiff or bald with age, though its flax drawstring fell to pieces as Bud pulled it. Carefully she shook out the contents – a sharpened bone, surely a knife, a necklace of polished black seeds, a handful of green parrot feathers, and a fishbone with a hole painstakingly bored in one end.

'It's a needle,' whispered Bud. Her face screwed up, and she stammered, 'It's so sad. Imagine a needle! They're like us, after all.'

They are? Who are? Nathan longed to hear what she thought, and at the same time was fiercely disinclined to listen.

'What's that?' cried Bud. 'I can hear something!'

They ran along the ledge and immediately saw the helicopter, far away against the valley's further wall, a silver grasshopper snuffling about the cliffs and tumbled rocks. After the breathing hush of the bush, its clatter was so familiar, so ordinary that Bud and Nathan choked with pure gratitude. They jumped and waved, rushed up and down the ledge, shrieked their heads off.

The craft slipped sideways, gained altitude, and wavered away over the far ridge.

'Well, they're looking for us, anyway,' said Nathan.

Twice before darkness fell they saw other helicopters, searching up and down valleys invisible to the children. Hope rose and vanished.

'They're looking in the wrong places,' said Bud miserably.

'Dad wouldn't have expected us to cut off towards Bedarra,' said Nathan. He didn't bother to mention that it was Bud who had gone that way and not himself.

'Is this Bedarra?' asked Bud, drearily.

'I guess so.'

Bud sounded even thinner and smaller than she looked. Her face was fuzzy white in the twilight. For already night was falling, and a chill mist ghosting up from the depths of the valley below.

The night was freezing. For a little while the rockface at their backs gave back the heat it had absorbed during the day, but after that the cold hung in the air like something solid. Their misery did not make things better between them. There was no reconciliation. Once Nathan suggested that if they sat back to back they might get a bit warmer, but Bud said she'd rather go and sit with the bones.

They shivered and suffered, wide awake between tormented drowsing. Owls called. Down in the valley animals squealed in the darkness. It was very dark; the moon cloud-covered.

'I keep thinking of – you know, that person. Why didn't the others, her friends, or her husband, come and save the baby, anyway?'

'Perhaps they couldn't find her. We haven't been found yet, either, not even with helicopters to help.'

'It must have been very lonely for her,' said Bud soberly.

There was a question Nathan had wanted to ask for hours. Now he did.

'Do you know what sort of . . . person . . . she was?'

'Sure,' said Bud, surprised. 'She was a yowie. Like on this T-shirt you gave me.'

Nathan wanted to ask how much his sister knew about yowies. He had known practically nothing himself until Fred, the Swedish boy, had bidden him goodbye with the laughing words, 'If I meet a yowie up there in the bush he will think I am a yowie, too, I am so large and awkward!'

When he returned to the motel, Nathan had hunted up the tourist information book he had bought in Coonabarabran. It had a lot about yowies, which it called mythical creatures, for the Warrumbungles were supposed to be a place they once inhabited. They were almost like giants, and ill-made like giants, too, hulking, flat-footed and clumsy, easily tricked. The youngest black hunter could frighten and drive away a yowie. Sometimes they killed them, too.

There had never been many of them. Perhaps they were a branch of the human species that could not cope very well, which was why they hid away in remote mountain ranges and impassable forests. They were peaceable and had no weapons, and in time they had vanished altogether.

The yowies were part of a myth. And yet theirs was also a sad story. Sad the way history was often sad.

'How did you hear about yowies, then?' Nathan asked his sister.

'The Japanese kids told me,' she replied. 'They have some kind of funny big creature in their mountains, too. You know, like Bigfoot in America.'

Nathan thought it was pretty weird that, like himself, Bud had to learn about yowies from people from overseas. He hadn't even heard about lace monitors, or the observatory at Siding Spring. He hoped Fred wouldn't go back to Sweden believing he was really dumb. But on the other hand he had had a strange experience. In fact, the more he thought about that first night, when he woke up in the car, the stranger his experience seemed.

He told Bud about it, the paws running over the car – paws that might easily have been timid hands exploring an interesting object from boot to bonnet. And then the terrific bump against the car, as if something or someone very massive had been startled and banged into it in the darkness.

'Oh, Nathan!' said Bud. 'You are lucky!'

The book said that yowies were curious. They hung around Aboriginal camps and watched from a distance. A few times they had stolen children or babies, just to have a good look at them. They always brought them back unharmed.

'Suppose some *have* survived! Around here. Just a few, keeping themselves secret.'

'From us,' said Bud angrily. 'Because we're dangerous.'

The feathers in the woman's dilly bag had been bright and soft. She hadn't died fifty years ago. Maybe only five or ten years ago. She might even have seen planes go over. How scared she would have been! But still the yowies hid, kept themselves secret.

Because we're dangerous, thought Nathan. That knowledge truly hurt him.

He fell asleep for a little while. When he awakened it was dawn. A peachy light ran along the battlements of the opposite side of the valley. He was frozen stiff and hurt all over. He felt a thousand years old.

Bud said, 'I can hear a helicopter somewhere.'

And there it was, a twinkle in the dawn sky, clattering up and down, busily looking in the wrong places, but the Riches knew it was just a matter of time before they were spotted.

Bud laughed. 'I bet Mum and Dad have made it up now that we've been lost!'

Nathan thought that was cruel. But it was probably true, too. And both things were characteristic of Bud, not that he'd known it before Sunday. In fact, he hadn't known anything about her except that she drove him nuts.

The children did not have to discuss the bones. They knew that if the skeletons were ever known about, that would be the beginning of the end of the yowies' hidden existence. It was easy to imagine the army of scientists, naturalists, greenies, TV crews that would invade the ancient Warrumbungles, the frantic publicity that always followed some unusual discovery.

'But if we throw them down into the valley they might be found some day.'

'Right,' said Nathan. 'But there's not much chance anyone else will accidentally fall on this ledge. Not for a hundred years, anyway. We'll push the bones back as far as we can and cover them.'

There was plenty of debris on the ledge. Together Bud and Nathan rolled the bones into the recess under the overhang and heaped branches and soil and dead leaves against them. Nathan caught Bud looking wistfully at the fishbone needle, but he shook his head.

'Put it back. We haven't seen anything. This is our secret.'

Each thought separately that now they had one thing in common, even if they never had anything else. And it was a good and rare thing, that would not be mentioned again as long as they lived.

The sound of the helicopter was louder now. Then the craft was overhead. Nathan and Bud rushed along the ledge. They tore off their T-shirts and waved them, madly shouting. The machine dodged away, returned, and hovered above, gently vibrating like a dragonfly about to pounce.

'There's Daddy! I can see Daddy!' shouted Bud.

Before very long a rope with a man on the end descended towards them.

WHAT KIND OF LADY WAS AUNTIE BEV?

IN THE BURDOCK FAMILY there were two people who enjoyed making their own soap opera, and two who didn't. Those who didn't were Wilmet Burdock and her father, Septimus. They spent a good deal of their time calmly observing Tiny Burdock, the girls' mother, and Cara, Willy's older sister, as one or the other rampaged around in a drama of tragedy, fury or excitement. Then Willy and Sep would go off and do their own things. Sep was a potter, an almost famous one. Willy was just any twelve-year-old, growing up and a bit undecided about it.

Tiny Burdock was a television actress, and always on the move. She was very pretty, and the size of a fairy, which gave her much satisfaction. She often pointed out to her daughters how gigantic they were. This threw Cara into sulks and did not matter at all to Willy. Tiny thought of herself as tenderhearted, sensitive as a little bird, but in reality she was as tough as old boots. Still, her family loved her. They did not want her to be different.

Tiny was away when Sep Burdock received the letter from his Aunt Beverley. He looked as if someone had hit him on the head. Willy was curious, but continued clearing the breakfast table. She knew he would tell her what was in the letter when he was ready.

'Where's Cara?' he asked.

'Upstairs squealing at a pimple on her chin,' answered Willy. She added that Cara intended to kill herself rather than go to school with such disfigurement.

'That's all right,' said Sep. 'As it happens, we have to visit Auntie Bev. All three of us. Today.'

Willy had never met Auntie Bev, and almost never thought of her. She frowned at her father.

'Not today. There's netball practice.'

'Today. She says so.'

Willy gazed at her father in amazement. 'Is she the queen?' she asked indignantly.

'Yes,' said Sep. 'Lord, I wish Tiny were home.'

He seemed quite shaken.

'Is she so awful, Dad?' asked Willy.

He considered. 'Not awful. More – well, I can't really say. Except for Christmas and birthday greetings we haven't been in touch for so long. Dress as nicely as you can, Willy. And tell Cara she's not to wear those pink jeans. They make her tail-end look like two pumpkins.'

When Cara heard about Auntie Bev's summons, she cried excitedly, 'Bet she's going to die!'

Willy thought that remark rather crude, but she understood what her sister meant. She thought about it as she put on her school uniform, which was smartly cut, and of a green which showed off her fair hair.

'Seeing we're the only relatives she has left,' said Cara, 'she'll leave us all her diamonds. I was born for diamonds, I know I was.'

'Dad said not to wear those pink pants because they make your . . .'

'Don't dare say it!' shuddered Cara. She flung on her cream pleated skirt and red jacket, adding red tights and shoes with heels. She put make-up over the spot on her chin, and small gold rings in her ears. She practised one or two charming expressions.

While this was going on, the black poodle sat in the doorway, his front paw raised in dismay. Coke knew about shoes. If the girls were putting on their town shoes, Coke knew he would be left alone all day, which he couldn't bear. Usually he had Sep to keep him company, for Sep worked at home. But Sep, too, had put on his going-out shoes. Coke uttered a loud melancholy groan.

'You'll have Cosy to play with,' Cara consoled him.

Coke quite liked the family cat, but she didn't like him. He groaned again.

'Well, I don't know what this is all about, Coke,' Willy explained as they left the room. 'But you needn't worry. You and I will stick together, no matter what happens.'

It was a four-hour drive to Aunt Bev's home. She lived in a handsome old house called Cherryvale.

'I expect she's very rich,' said Cara.

'I guess so,' replied her father. 'She was a very successful businesswoman before she retired. She must be about seventy-eight,' he mused, 'much older than my father would be if he were alive.'

'Oh, poor her,' said Cara.

But Willy said dreamily: 'What a lot of wonderful things she must have to remember.'

They drove south through golden countryside, beside a dawdling river. The long silty flats were dense with yellow poplars. Willy watched a pelican glide in to set down on the river, cautiously remaining a leg's length above the water for ages before he landed. Willy liked that. The pelican was not one to rush things, and neither was she.

Cherryvale came out of the trees all of a sudden. It had many gables and white-railed verandahs, and seven blackberry-brick chimneys. The garden gently sloped to the river, and at the end was a crumbling jetty with splayed legs. Cara said it looked like a mansion from a historical film. Cherryvale did have an other-times look, mused Willy. She felt she could, if she tried, blow it away, back into the golden light from which it had come.

'It's unreal,' sighed Cara. 'But surely Auntie Bev doesn't do all the housework? I mean, she's so terribly antique and everything.'

'No, I don't,' replied Auntie Bev, when she was asked the same question half an hour later. 'I have two maids and a man for the car and the garden. And until recently my housekeeper, Mrs Stannage.'

Auntie Bev unnerved Cara, who had done nothing but show off since she entered the drawing-room, twittering on about the chandeliers and the black marble fireplace, curtseying before a tall greenish mirror, and interrupting the conversation with giggles and winsome squeaks. Wilmet had kicked her once or twice.

'Oh,' she cried now, 'but where's Mrs Stannage? I thought housekeepers always answered the door looking black and murderous. They do on TV.'

'Mrs Stannage died two months ago,' answered her aunt, and she flicked Cara a look that made her great-niece shut up and sit down. Auntie Bev inclined to such glances. Willy had rather expected her to be a vague pussy-shaped old bundle, but she was not like that at all. She was very thin and small. Though she moved as though she were in pain, Willy had the impression that it was not long since she had been nimble and quick. She wore a designer tracksuit of dull blue silk, and several costly-looking gold chains.

Willy did not care about gold chains. She looked with

pleasure around the room which had everything she felt
easy with, a dim Persian rug, many books, a collection
of ruby glass, and enormous potplants. Almost trees,
they were. Willy thought that a person might expect
birds to fly out of them, gaily coloured birds.

'Would you care to look through the house, Wilmet?'
asked Auntie Bev, gently.

Willy jumped up, beaming, and Cara jumped up too.

'Not you, Cara,' said their aunt.

Willy was glad she first saw Cherryvale by herself.
Everywhere she went it was as though she had been
there before. The house liked her.

'So there you are!' she imagined it saying.

The house made its rooms warmer for her. It wafted
its curtains aside and showed her the river fringed with
willows, the low hills covered with wind-bitten bush. It
breathed out delicious odours, clove and violet and
cedar. Its furniture fitted it hand in glove, and the faded
rugs knew their place and never dominated the room.

Slowly Willy drifted downstairs. The stairs were lighted by an oval window of coloured glass, which showed
a dove sitting amongst white and yellow flowers.

In a happy dream she returned to the drawing-room.

'We're going to live here!' shrieked Cara the moment
she entered. 'Oh, isn't it sensational?'

Willy nodded, smiling at Auntie Bev.

She sat down and listened to the old lady, and sometimes her father, when Sep felt he ought to make things
clearer.

'As long as Mrs Stannage was alive, I could manage,'
explained Auntie Bev. 'But now she is gone, and the
maids are elderly and wish to retire, so I think it's time
for me to change my lifestyle.'

She was going into a retirement home. She had made arrangements for her nephew Septimus to take over Cherryvale, with enough money for its maintenance. On her death he became her sole heir.

'The old stables would convert into an excellent pottery studio, I believe, Sep,' she said.

The three younger Burdocks were speechless, even Cara.

'I wanted to see you just to reassure myself that the arrangement will benefit us all. I wish I could have met your wife, Sep. Lenore, is it not?'

'Yes, but the name never took. We call her Tiny.'

'I have seen her on television. Exquisite. So *neat*.'

Cara jabbed an elbow into Willy. When at home Tiny was so untidy she had raised muddle to an art form. Sep and Willy were the opposite. Every time Tiny departed interstate they had a mighty clear-up.

Auntie Bev inquired whether they had pets.

'There's Coke,' said Willy. 'He's really Monsieur Coco; he's a poodle. But he's wonderfully good inside houses, truly.'

'Yes, poodles are gentlemen,' agreed Auntie Bev. 'But the cat?'

'Just a cat. You know.'

Auntie Bev drew in her nostrils and said, 'Then she must look after herself.'

Willy thought that Auntie Bev had a fascinating face, wrinkled, of course, but sharply elegant. It was ivory-coloured, like a statue's. Willy felt it was an old-fashioned face, like Richard III's, or someone else in a history book. But when Auntie Bev said that about Cosy, she looked different. For a moment the stunning blue trouser suit seemed so out of place, Willy felt a twinge of uneasiness. It was there, it was gone, and she forgot it.

So they said goodbye and went home. A few days later Tiny returned, all fragrance and jingly ear-bobs and gladness to see them again. They were thrilled to see her and give her the news. Not for a moment had anyone thought she might object to living in lovely Cherryvale, and she didn't.

'Are there really cherries? Cherry trees?'

'Yes, a whole avenue.'

'When they're in bloom we'll have a cherry blossom party. Simply hundreds of people!'

Septimus and Willy gave each other a stealthy glance. They could imagine who the hundreds of people would be – gorgeous yelling creatures from films and theatre.

'Frightening the swans and pelicans,' mourned Wilmet silently.

'And what about school for my girls?'

'No problem,' said Sep. 'There's a super one inland at Balgarret, and I've already rung them to see if there's room for our two. It's a fairly long drive, morning and afternoon, but I'll be chauffeur. We're a two-car family now. Auntie Bev is leaving the Rover.'

'Fantastic!' breathed Cara.

'There's another old house next door to Cherryvale,' said Willy happily. 'It's called Glenella, and the old man who owns it has a huge pond, and there are ducks on it, coloured ducks! Auntie Bev said they're Chinese.'

Cara did not hear a word.

'And there's the river, Mum!' she raved. 'Imagine publicity pictures of you amongst the willows! And maybe we can get a boat. So trendy just now.'

'If my pots sell,' said Sep wistfully. He was one of

those potters who win prizes at exhibitions but not expensive commissions.

'They will now,' said Willy.

She sat beside him in the pottery. He often waited there for the last stages of the kiln's cooling down, sitting quietly, moulding a lump of clay in his fingers, looking absentminded.

'Dad,' she said, 'do you like Auntie Bev?'

'I don't know,' he answered. 'I don't really know her. What do you feel, Willy?'

Wilmet considered. 'I don't know, either. But she liked me, I think.'

Within a few weeks Septimus received a letter from Beverley Burdock's solicitor, a Mr Paling. The letter contained the deed to the Cherryvale property, and the documents of transfer. Everything was in order.

Sep was instructed that the house was now locked and vacant, as Auntie Bev had departed for her retirement home.

'She's the dearest duckie in the world,' sang Tiny, 'and I'm going to phone her at once to thank her. I'll tell her I'll look after Cherryvale just like a teeny Mary Poppins.'

Willy and Sep, who were packing pots and pans in the kitchen, raised their eyebrows at each other. Cara was out, as she had been every spare moment for a week, saying tragic farewells to friends.

'I'd like a word with Aunt Bev too,' Sep called to Tiny in the hall. But Tiny flew back, big-eyed, hands to her cheeks.

'She isn't there!'

'Montello Sunset Home?'

'They've never heard of her!'

Tiny produced a shower of tears that made no difference at all to her face. She blinked through them as through diamonds.

'No Miss Burdock has made a booking there! Oh, Sep!'

'Just some misunderstanding. Don't cry, love.'

Sep rang Mr Paling, who contacted Montello, and then the Burdocks once more. Auntie Bev seemed to have disappeared.

'Somewhat puzzling, I confess,' Mr Paling said, in his chill way.

'What about the servants?' asked Sep. 'The old gardener chap? Would they know anything?'

The old gardener had retired a month before Aunt Bev closed the house. He was already back in England, whence he had come long before. The two maids, elderly cousins, who had bought a retirement apartment in Sydney, had also left Cherryvale before Aunt Bev. They were bewildered.

'But of course she must be at Montello,' they insisted. 'She spoke of it so many times. We meant to visit her this coming Sunday.'

The older one broke down. 'She was so generous. Always so kind to us. Oh, dear, poor Miss Burdock, where could she be?'

Where *could* an old lady be? There was a great fuss, which Cara enjoyed tremendously, and gained Tiny mention in all the TV columns. Willy and Coke retired to a corner of the pottery, puzzled and upset.

In spite of police inquiries there was no sign of Auntie Bev, and never was again. Her solicitor said cautiously that perhaps she had a dizzy spell on that old Cherryvale jetty, and slipped into the river.

'Those dangerous old planks,' he murmured. 'And the current runs swiftly there. Whirled away out to sea . . . perhaps her own decision, all very regrettable.'

Sep went away not knowing whether Mr Paling had meant that she had drowned herself or not.

'She said she was going to change her lifestyle, that's all,' argued Willy. 'You know very well she'd hate jumping in the cold river in winter.'

'But why mislead us all about booking in at Montello?' sighed Tiny, clawing over the heap of shoes in the bottom of her wardrobe. 'Oh, where are my butterfly boots, my greeny ones, do come and find them, Cara sweetie.'

'I'm not going to grow old,' announced Cara, scuffling amidst the shoes. 'The moment I turn forty I shall O.D.'

'Good idea,' said Willy crossly. 'And you'd better start packing your things or you *will* be forty before it's done.'

There was no obstacle in the family's moving into Cherryvale, as the gift had been made before Aunt Bev's disappearance or death. So the move was made. The winter wattle was blooming; there were a few snowdrops under the camellia hedges.

When Sep unlocked the front door, warm fresh air blew out.

'You'd never think the house has been shut up for weeks,' marvelled Willy. Coke stepped in and stood still, dilating his black leather nostrils, picking up all the odours of a strange place. Then he gave one of his gusty sighs, and walked in confidently.

Cara opened Cosy's basket. In a hideous temper the

big cream cat leaped to a stairpost, crouching there cursing.

'Silly old pudda,' cooed Tiny. Cosy lashed out and scratched her hand. But it needed more than a cat's huffiness to upset Tiny, who raced from room to room, sucking her hand between cries of wonder and joy.

'The furniture! The rugs! Oh, that blissful Auntie Bev! Cara, run down and see if there are buds on the cherry trees, I just can't wait for our party. Oh, what a shame I have to go away again!'

'Must you, Tiny?' Sep sounded unhappy.

'I must, I must. I'll have to leave things to you and the girls and whizz off. Sep dearest, I'll miss you madly as always, but there are these nightmare retakes, and the film audition. Oh, it's so unfair!'

Within two days she had hopped into the Rover and sped off to Sydney.

In spite of Cherryvale's seven bedrooms, Cara and Willy decided to continue sharing. They were used to it, and besides, they liked each other's company. They chose a bedroom with five odd-cornered walls, and one of the gables, windowed all round and looking over big trees and a sheen of river. As Cherryvale was so old, there were no built-ins anywhere except in the kitchen, but one corner of the girls' new bedroom was filled, floor to ceiling, with a carved wooden cupboard which would do very well as a wardrobe.

'It's so big you could let it as a studio flat,' laughed Cara, tugging at the tall heavy doors.

Suddenly they opened, and the girls saw that the cupboard still contained clothes. Dresses and skirts hung in clear plastic covers, and shoes stood in order on racks –

high heels, walking heels, boots and evening slippers. On the high shelves above were boxes, labelled SCARVES, STOCKINGS, BELTS and so on. It was so different from their mother's wardrobe, where everything hung on the floor in heaps, that they could scarcely believe it.

Willy's heart gave a sick kind of jump. 'She didn't even take her clothes! Maybe she *did* drown herself in the river.'

But Cara didn't hear. She twitched dresses off their hangers and tried them against herself.

'Wow, look at this! A mini skirt! I've never seen a genuine old-time mini.'

'Oh, please don't, Cara,' begged her sister. 'She wouldn't like you pulling her clothes around. Oh, put them back, Cara, it's such awful cheek . . .'

Now Cara had taken a silver slipper from the rack, and was trying to jam her big sneaker foot into it. The sight was so brutal Willy wept. She wasn't an easy crier like her mother and Cara. Tears hurt her. Her face turned scarlet and her mouth opened to let out a big gulp. Cara was amazed.

'Cool it, cool it. I won't. It doesn't fit, anyway. You truly weird me out, Willy. Fancy crying over the clothes of a dead old lady!'

'Maybe she isn't dead,' protested Willy.

'Okay,' said Cara good-naturedly. 'But we'll have to get them out of the way, or we won't have enough space.'

'I'll do it!' offered Willy eagerly.

Cara grinned. 'You really are a freaky character,' she said.

She bounced out and phoned her mother, who adored

142

her family and liked to hear from them every day. Cara was not surprised that Tiny was having a temperament. Her professional life was over, she said between sobs. She had misgivings about the audition; a fiendish director had blown her up in front of everyone; and she had been written out of her latest soap opera.

'They won't even give me a decent death scene,' she wailed. 'I'm to be phased out in a car smash. Crash, bang, and then the cat-food commercial. The producer wants the role for his totty.'

Tiny always referred to people's girlfriends as their totties. For a long time Cara had thought it a proper word. Now she asked, 'How can the character come back if she's been killed off in a car smash?'

'She comes back as a different person, having had plastic surgery. Did you ever! And his totty is twice as big as me. I mean, you can change faces with surgery, I guess, but what about hips? Hers belong on a casserole.'

'Cheer up,' said Cara, when her mother paused for another sob. 'One day the cherries will bloom, and guess what? Willy and I found a cupboardful of hilarious old dresses and hats and things. Now you can make your party fancy dress!'

Meanwhile Wilmet had set about her task. The cupboard was so large she could easily push Auntie Bev's clothes along to the end of the rail without squashing them. Willy thought Aunt Bev would prefer that to having them moved to another room. She knew enough from her mother, a fashion fanatic, that these dresses represented the styles of many years. Had Auntie Bev been as old as all that, wondered Willy, peeking through the plastic cover at a 1920s dress hung with beaded fringes in long diagonals. Then there was an ankle-length brown skirt with a ruffle at the hem. And a coffee-coloured lace blouse with a high boned collar to go with it. Hadn't girls worn that kind of thing at the beginning of the century? Tiny had been in a play set about that time; Willy remembered her mother complaining bitterly about a stiff sailor hat that belonged with a costume like that. But still, what Auntie Beverley had worn wasn't Willy's business, so she fetched a chair and climbed up to push the boxes of accessories to the back of the shelf. Now she could see the carvings clearly; they were of fox heads, oak leaves and bunches of berries.

One of the boxes fell to the floor, and the lid shot off. Willy got down to fetch it. It was a round hat box. It was full of oddments that seemed to have been collected together for mending, or even throwing away – broken necklaces, gloves with worn fingertips, a fur neckpiece, bald in spots, and a fur hat like a hairy teacosy. Willy tried on the hat. It came down over her nose and smelled of perfume and dust.

Cokie strolled in and set up a demented barking. It was unlike him, so Willy took off the hat and said, 'It's only me, you old twit.'

Still barking, he backed out of the room. Willy put the hat back into the box. Just then her Dad called from downstairs.

'Hey, Willy! Want to come next door to visit Mr Glendower?'

Willy longed to have a closer look at Glenella and the

ducks on the pond. Hastily she pushed the box to the back of the cupboard and threw its lid after it. She thought she'd sort out the contents another time.

'Coming, Cara?'

'Good heavens, no!' said Cara, settling down for a good long chat on the phone.

'We've been invited to tea,' added Sep. Cara didn't hear. She was too busy telling her mother how they had been interviewed by the principal of Balgarret College and how much better an impression they would have made if their father had driven up in the Rover instead of the family rust-bucket.

'Rather a snob, our Cara,' said Sep, as they went up Glenella's weedless drive.

'I like her a bit, though,' said Willy. Sep nodded.

Mr Glendower was eighty at least. He had a houseful of antiques and a pleasant, elderly housekeeper.

'I like your ducks *very much*,' said Willy, hoping to please the old man. She took a scone and was careful not to drop crumbs.

'See you have a cat!' announced Mr Glendower.

'A dog, too!' added the housekeeper, pouring out tea.

'Yes, we like animals,' said Sep cheerfully. But Willy at once saw what Mr Glendower was worried about.

'Oh,' she said, 'Cosy would never dream – she's the cat, you know. A British cream. She's very lazy, and never, never hunts. Your ducks are quite safe.'

'Dog, then! Eh? What about the dog?' said Mr Glendower, chopping out the words.

'Cokie is a homebody,' explained Sep. 'Always under our feet. A very civilised dog. Never wanders.'

'Please, Mr Glendower,' said Willy earnestly. 'Don't

145

worry. But we understand. Dad and I'd be just the same if we had gorgeous ducks like yours. And I'd like to go and see them, if I may.'

'Well, then,' said Mr Glendower, relaxing. His knobby hand tremblingly pushed a plate of cake towards Sep. 'You're not eating, my boy. Mrs Clay, please take the young lady to feed the ducks.'

At dinner that night Willy could scarcely do more than nibble, she was so stuffed with cake and scones, and, more than that, with impressions of the house next door.

'Come on, Willy,' said Cara at last, 'tell us about the ducks.'

Willy knew Cara didn't care at all about the ducks. She was being social.

'They're coloured, and rather big,' said Willy at last. She did not feel like telling Cara that the ducks looked as if they had waddled out of a Chinese painting. What's more, they were agreeable birds, not pecking or clamouring as hens would, as they flocked to Mrs Clay's feet, but peeping sociably, giving each other room.

'They're a very rare, ancient breed. They're called Wei River ducks,' explained Mrs Clay. 'And here's their husband. His name is Yang. You must call him Honourable Person Yang.'

The drake came straight to Mrs Clay, the ducks moving aside politely. Yang was a magnificent bird with an opalescent jade neckband and a tuft on his tail. He eyed Willy, decided she was not dangerous, and opened wide his clipped wings. Stretching his neck, he bowed his head to the ground. Willy was enraptured.

'What does he mean by that?' she whispered.

'I don't know,' said the housekeeper. 'It's just a duck-ish thing.'

Willy liked that. She made up her mind that later she too would keep ducks, and be able to observe their duckish ways as much as she wanted.

'Watch this,' said Mrs Clay. The drake, having finished eating, had waddled to her feet. Mrs Clay picked him up carefully, one hand under his broad keel-like breast, the other under his webs.

'You must always be careful how you pick up a duck. They feel uneasy off the ground. Well, Honourable Person Yang, I bid you good day and a long life.'

The drake delicately tweaked at the gold ring in Mrs Clay's ear. Willy was amazed how gently he could use that wide, clumsy bill.

'Oh, if only he would do that to me, one day,' she said. 'No wonder Mr Glendower loves them so much.' She knew what Mrs Clay was thinking and added, 'And you needn't worry ever. About Cokie and Cosy, I mean.'

'Mr Glendower's family have bred Wei River ducks for 120 years, ever since this house was built,' said Mrs Clay. 'They've won prizes all over Australia. But more than that, they are part of Glenella, and the family treasures.'

Willy understood very well. She said no more to Cara, who was, anyway, enlarging on the subject of totties and their disastrous effect upon the careers of genuine TV actresses.

Willy had never been so contented in her life. She loved her room so much she couldn't wait to go to bed. Then she couldn't wait to wake up, so she could walk through the house and know it was satisfied with her. She looked forward to attending school at Balgarret. Everything was perfect except Cosy.

The big cat was still being difficult. She refused to settle down. She wandered around, wailing, and once Cara found her on her bed, making the terrible boiling kettle sound of an enraged cat at nothing at all.

'Do cats have a menopause?' she asked her father.

'Don't be nutty,' said Willy. 'You know she's desexed. She's probably homesick for our other house.'

Cosy went on being solitary and unfriendly, lurking on window sills and under furniture, coming out only for food, which she ate quickly and angrily.

'Just wait till I get the studio in order, and I'll take her to the vet for a check,' promised Sep.

The nights were cold, and Willy sometimes found it hard to fall asleep. In the past Cokie had usually slept with her. He was the warmest creature to cuddle as she drifted into dreams. When she turned over, he turned over; when she woke up, he was already awake, his large intelligent eyes fixed on her face, waiting for her to join him in the new day.

'Where are you, Coke?' she whispered.

A faint groan answered her from the doorway.

'What *are* you doing out there all by yourself?' she asked, getting out of bed. Cokie was curled up near the doorway. He trembled with cold.

'What's the matter with you, goofy dog? Come to bed at once.'

She picked him up and carried him in. But the moment she put him on the bed he jumped off and flickered out of the room like a shadow. Willy was slightly offended.

Next day she mentioned it to her father. He was busily conferring with a workman over the conversion of the stables into a pottery.

'Maybe he just had a stomach-ache,' said Sep. 'You know how he likes to be fairly close to the dog-door when he knows he'll have to go out. He's so good that way.'

'There isn't a dog-door here,' pointed out Willy. 'And Coke knows that. He would have wakened me or someone if he wanted to go outside in a hurry.'

'We must have one cut,' said Sep absently, missing the point altogether. 'Now, Steve, with regard to the skylight . . .'

Willy went away and found Coke. She sat down beside him and gently scratched the edges of his long fringed ears, which he loved.

'Now, let's get this straight, Coke,' she said. 'I know that if you don't want to sleep in our bedroom you have a good reason, so that's all I'll say about it. But please remember that I'm always on your side. And Cara is too. Okay?'

Balgarret was the best of schools. Cara immediately became popular, not only because their mother was well known, but because she herself was amusing and clever. In a week she had flocks of friends. Willy thought she'd look around a bit more amongst the other students before she decided.

'Willy likes to browse,' Sep explained to Tiny when she rang from Adelaide. Tiny was always anxious about her girls being popular. She thought if they were not queens of their respective classes they were nowhere.

Cara invited her friends home to Cherryvale to stay the night. There were so many spare bedrooms this was no trouble. But Sep got tired of chauffeuring four or five girls to school so often, and the springs of the rust-bucket felt less and less springy.

'Why ever don't you get yourself decent wheels, Mr Burdock?' asked one of Cara's pushier friends.

'Because I'm eccentric,' answered Sep. Willy, squeezed between two overlapping girls, thought that was good. The pushy one accepted it at once.

'Oh, that's because you're an artist,' she explained kindly. 'My father's a musician and he's raving mad. And I mean raving.'

While she went on about how exactly her father raved, Willy thought of *her* new friends, Mr Glendower and Mrs Clay. She had found a little space in the hawthorn hedge which separated the two properties, and she was allowed to slither through and visit. She often accompanied the housekeeper when she fed the ducks, and sometimes she talked awhile with Mr Glendower, an interesting old man, though he tired quickly.

'Run along, lass,' he'd say. 'My bones are grumbling.'

Willy supposed that bones did when a person was eighty, and she was sorry for Mr Glendower.

Neither Mrs Clay or the old gentleman had again mentioned Cosy or Cokie, and their possible danger to the ducks. They were well-bred people, and trusted in the Burdocks' assurances.

But suddenly everything went wrong.

Willy came home from Glenella to find Cara and two of her friends trying on Auntie Bev's clothes.

Almost the moment she squeezed through the haw-

thorn hedge into Cherryvale's garden, she knew
something wasn't right. For a start, the kitchen chimney,
which carried away the fumes from the slow-combustion
stove in the entrance hall, was smoking in an unusual
way. There was far too much smoke, greenish smoke at
that, whirling and twisting into a thick spiral. Willy
sprinted for the house. She was sure something awful
had happened to that stove. The house might catch fire!

She burst through the front door, to find the stove
glowing placidly in its customary manner.

'There must have been some kind of funny wind
above the roof,' thought Willy, perplexed.

Shrieks of laughter sounded from upstairs, Willy
didn't much like Colette and Steffie, and they scarcely
noticed her at all. She glanced about; everything seemed
in order. In the kitchen Cosy crouched under the table
hissing.

'Honestly, Cosy, I think you're going dotty,' said
Willy.

The house felt different. In spite of the stove, it was
chilly and unwelcoming. The curtains hung dankly as if
they were a hundred years old. Rugs lay crookedly. The
lovely light that filtered down the stairway from the
coloured glass window had turned cobwebby and grey.
And Steffie and Colette and Cara, giggling their heads
off, sounded like faraway fierce birds.

Willy had an overwhelming urge to be with someone,
even fat Colette and freaky old Steff. She raced upstairs.
There were the three of them, big girls all, jammed into
Auntie Bev's dresses, wearing her hats and necklaces,
posturing before the mirror and each other.

'You take those things off!' spat Willy. It was almost

as if Auntie Bev herself had spoken in that crystal voice of hers. The three girls stared, startled, clutching their finery about them.

'What's with you?' demanded Steffie.

'Get them off at once!' shouted Willy. She yelled so loudly that Sep, cleaning up the new pottery, heard her and thought he'd better go and see what was happening. Coke, who had been keeping him company, streaked for the house.

'Come off it, Willy,' laughed Cara. 'We're just having fun dressing up! Right?'

'They're Aunt Beverley's clothes, she wouldn't want great lumps like you squeezing into them. Look at that blouse Colette's got on, she's burst all the buttons, the creep!'

'Pay no attention,' advised Steffie. 'That's the best way with kids like her. Honestly, Cara, you ought to keep her in line.'

But Cara looked embarrassed, even guilty. Slowly she began to remove the long blue crepe dress with the dipping hemline, the ropes of pearly beads.

'Maybe we shouldn't have,' she began. Coke, sitting in the doorway, lifted his head and uttered a hair-raising howl. Colette tore off the blouse, and jerked down the placket of the skirt.

'Bloody thing, it hasn't even got a zip!'

The skirt ripped down the side seam. Colette sneered at Willy.

'Oh, big deal! Here take the stupid rags if you're so keen on them.' She tossed the torn skirt at Willy, and her friend Steff contemptuously threw the fur hat she had been wearing after it. Sep caught it as he entered the room.

'They've . . . they've . . . what ever would Auntie Bev say . . .?' Willy choked. Sep glanced around the room, littered with clothing, shoes and accessories.

Steffie shot behind the opened wardrobe door and hauled on her own clothes. Colette followed her, saying loudly, 'Cara said it was all right. She said the old turkey was dead.'

'If you mean Miss Burdock, there's no proof of that,' replied Sep soberly. 'Cara, you haven't done the right thing here.'

Cara longed to say something smart but she could not think of a single crack. Her father looked so serious she had genuine misgivings. Besides, she really hated the trashy way her friends had flung Auntie Bev's clothes at Willy.

'No,' she admitted at last.

'Oh, wow! listen to the fink!' jeered Steffie.

'What a fuss about nothing!' said Colette. 'I've had enough of this, I'm going home.'

Cara was red-faced, fumbling out words.

'I don't blame you girls,' said Sep. 'You are welcome to stay for the weekend as arranged, if you wish.'

But they didn't wish, and Sep drove them home.

Cara helped Willy put the garments back into their plastic envelopes, roll up the belts and scarves and tidy them into their boxes. The girls had spent hours dragging the clothes carelessly on and off, and many garments were damaged and crumpled. Cara felt furious with her friends and even more furious with herself.

'It was a sleazy thing to do,' she thought. 'And I'll tell Colette and Steffie so on Monday. It's true that they coaxed me, but I shouldn't have given in.'

'Even Auntie Bev's old fur hat!' raged Willy, tossing it

into the hat box. She put the box back in the cupboard. 'Tearing things. Pulling them around. Calling Aunt Bev a turkey. The stinkers! It's because of Auntie Bev we're here at Cherryvale, and Dad has a proper studio and Mum has the Rover . . .'

Cara began to cry. Amongst all the sobs and sniffs Willy made out a few words.

'You didn't!' she said, aghast. 'Not Mum!'

'Yes, I did. Mum was miserable because she'd had a lousy day and I thought it would cheer her up to know she could have a ripper fancy-dress party instead of just an ordinary one.'

Willy thought about it. 'Well, she won't, when we explain things to her.'

'Yes, she will,' wailed Cara. 'She adored the idea and you know how determined she is.'

Willy scowled at her sister. Then she said, 'Well, maybe Dad will be able to kid her out of it.'

She didn't feel this was likely.

'Please don't mention it to Dad,' begged Cara. 'I'll tell him tomorrow. I feel so shattered just now.'

Cara had her mother's ability to appear pale and fragile at will. Sep said it was some trick of holding the breath, but when Wilmet tried it all that happened was that she turned crimson and almost burst. She thought it was all just plain devilment.

Cara looked at her pathetically, as though she were about to swoon away with repentance and sorrow, and Willy gave in as usual.

Before she went to bed she went down to the cherry avenue and anxiously felt along the twigs. They were as bare as sticks, but she could make out tiny bumps on the wood.

'Still,' she thought, 'it's a very cold winter. Blooming may be late this year. Mum may be too busy. Then she'll forget about her fancy-dress party.'

She heard distant voices from next door. Mrs Clay had checked that the ducks were snug for the night and was telling old Mr Glendower about it.

'One day,' Willy told Coke, 'Honourable Person Yang will nibble *my* ears, too. But of course he will never replace you as my closest friend.'

A pet-port had been cut in the kitchen door, and Coke dived through it gracefully. Cosy cursed him as he ambled past, but he paid no attention. He had given up sleeping outside the girls' door. Cara had put his rug near the stove in the hall, and he seemed contented enough there.

In the night Cara awakened. She heard a soft shuffling sound.

'Is that you, Cokie?' she muttered drowsily. 'Come on, boy, jump up!'

But no dog jumped nimbly on the bed to snuggle down beside her.

'Don't then,' said Cara.

The slithering began again. Now it seemed to be in the upstairs hall. It was the merest suggestion of sound, possibly Cosy come out of her sulks to chase a cockroach. Cara drifted into dreams again.

During the night there was a sudden hullabaloo from Coke. He seemed to be in the garden. Sep awoke with a start, lurched out of bed, and threw up the window.

'Shut up, Coke!' he roared in a whisper. 'Damn it, he must be after a possum.' When he heard a shrill yelp he was sure of it. If Coke had cornered a possum it had landed a swipe on him somewhere. The commotion had upset the ducks, too, for there was an outburst of quacking.

Sep whistled for Coke three or four times but there was no response. The night was icy cold, the wind sharp as knives, so Sep closed the window and jumped back into bed.

'Probably woken everyone up,' he grumbled. He looked at the clock. Only five past four, not worth trying to sleep again. He turned his thoughts to the new glaze he was working on, a faint peach with a lilac underlay.

'If it works out, I'll call it the Cherryvale. No, I won't, I'll call it the Beverley.'

All at once, he felt warm and sleepy. He dozed off, hardly hearing in the distance the outcry of the Chinese ducks.

At half-past six Sep was already in the pottery, studying the formula for the new glaze. At once he saw where he could change it for the better.

Though it was Saturday, Cara and Willy both went downstairs early, Willy putting on the kettle and Cara grumpy and not looking forward to telling her father about the fancy-dress party.

'Where's Coke?'

Toast crusts were Cokie's morning treat. He could smell them from the bottom of the garden. Cara went to the back door and called. No Cokie.

'I thought I heard him barking in the night,' she said. 'It was after Cosy was chasing that cockroach around the hall.'

'Cosy is afraid of cockroaches,' said Willy, making the tea. 'You were dreaming.'

Sep came up from the studio, rubbing his hands together, his breath in white clouds.

'Wasn't Coke with you?' asked Cara.

But Sep hadn't seen him. He told the girls about the disturbance in the early hours. Willy was puzzled. It wasn't like the black poodle to go out in the freezing darkness to chase a possum. But before she could say so, the phone rang. Sep was sure it was Tiny calling him.

'Maybe she's coming home early!'

But in a moment the smile had left his face. 'Mrs Clay!' he said in surprise. And then: 'Yes, of course I'll be there at once.'

'What's wrong, Dad?' faltered Cara, because it was plain something *was* wrong.

Sep threw on his anorak and scarf. 'The old man's had a turn of some kind. I'll drive him and Mrs Clay to Balgarret hospital.' At the door he halted for a moment to say: 'Something got in amongst his birds last night, killed several. They think it was Coke.'

He was gone.

Willy quavered, 'It *was not*! Cokie wouldn't hurt a fly.'

'Of course he wouldn't!' cried Cara. 'But where is he?'

They dressed hurriedly, and were halfway across the garden before Willy even thought of poor Mr Glendower, now on his way to the hospital. No wonder he'd had a turn, he loved those ducks so much.

The two girls stood horrified beside the pond. Most of the ducks were hiding in the long reedy grass. Willy could hear their timid piping. But nearby lay several soft heaps of feathers, including Yang the drake. As with the others, his neck had been broken. Willy began to sob. 'I bet he put up a fight for the flock. Oh, he was so beautiful! He loved Mrs Clay, he used to bow to her.'

'Knock it off, Willy!' ordered Cara. 'We have to think of Coke now.'

'But where is he?' choked Willy. She tried to be calm, but as they crawled through the hole in the hedge, her tears broke out once more. It was that which brought Coke out of his hiding place. He had never been able to bear humans crying.

'Coke!' gasped Cara. 'What has *happened* to you?'

Coke had holed up underneath the house. He was covered with dirt and cobwebs and smeared with blood. The girls' hearts sank when they saw that. Coke's tail and ears were down; he was exhausted, beaten to the ground.

'We know you didn't do anything, dearest dog,' declared Cara. That made Willy feel better. She blew her nose and stopped crying. She had been all of a heap with distress but with Cara beside her, she knew she could tackle most problems.

They examined Coke.

'Just look there!' said Cara triumphantly.

The blood came from a wound on his nose. He had two on his leg and another on his neck. They looked like small bites. They bore him inside and gave him an egg beaten in milk, to restore him after his mysterious ordeal. Then they carefully washed and disinfected his wounds. Coke perked up a little; he liked having a fuss made of him.

'Dad thought Coke went out after a possum,' said

Willy, 'but have you ever heard of a possum biting anyone?'

'Maybe it was a wild cat,' suggested Cara. 'And it attacked the ducks and Coke went to their rescue!'

'That's more like Coke,' said Willy stoutly. 'He's so brave.'

'But suppose Mr Glendower goes on believing Coke did it!' worried Cara. 'Those Wei River ducks are so valuable, and Mr Glendower is rapt in them. Suppose he tells the police?'

Willy could not answer. What *did* happen to dogs accused of killing other people's ducks? She hugged Coke protectively.

Mr Glendower's heart attack had been slight, and he was kept in hospital only a week. As soon as he was permitted to do so, Septimus visited him.

'It wasn't our poodle, you know,' he said quietly.

'Don't talk to me!' said Mr Glendower, glaring feebly.

'It must have been something else,' said Sep desperately. 'Coke himself has several deep bites.'

'Prissed-up fool of a dog!' ground out Mr Glendower. 'You gave me your word, Burdock!'

Sep waited until the old man's hurried breathing had calmed.

'I'm telling you the truth, Mr Glendower. What creature attacked your birds I don't know, but it was not Coke. And, I have to say this, those ducks would always have been safer in a pen.'

'What for?' demanded Mr Glendower fiercely. 'You think anyone around here would harm them? Proud of the Glenella ducks, the district is!'

He lay back panting, and Sep was upset to see a tear slipping from under a withered eyelid.

159

'My Yang,' said Mr Glendower. 'Pedigree as long as my arm!'

'Mr Glendower,' Sep said gently, 'won't you let me put up some kind of pen to keep the rest of them safe, at least until you go home and decide for yourself?'

'Fat lot of good that will do now!' croaked the old man. He said no more.

Sep picked up a roll of chickenwire in Balgarret, and fenced in a portion of the Glenella pond.

Mrs Clay was red-eyed.

'Please believe me, Mrs Clay,' said Sep, 'Mr Glendower wouldn't listen to me, but truly, it wasn't our Coke. The girls even think that Coke tried to fight off whatever it was that raided the ducks. A wildcat, maybe, or a fox?' he added hopefully.

'I've never seen a fox or a wildcat around here in my life,' replied the housekeeper, 'and I've been with Mr Glendower for thirty-two years.'

'But Mrs Clay,' began Septimus. She shook her head.

'He's the only dog nearby, and you did say he was hiding when the girls found him. That sounds like a guilty dog to me. The whole thing has hit the old gentleman very hard. And myself as well.'

She said good day and closed the door. Glumly, Sep took his wire cutters and the remains of the chickenwire and went down the drive, just in time to see the Rover scoot between the gateposts of Cherryvale.

Tiny Burdock came home a waif, thrown aside by the world. Even though she had more or less worn the edges off the role by the time the girls returned from school, she still looked wan, a strand of hair wisped over her shoulder, her eyelids were almost too weary to lift.

'Oh, my darlings,' she whispered. 'I've so longed for you all.'

By bending her knees a little, she managed to get her head on Cara's shoulder.

'So you flaked out in the audition?' said Cara.

Tiny snapped back her head. 'You are the most unfeeling girl! Really I can't imagine how you happen to be my daughter!'

'Cheer up, Mum,' said Cara briskly. 'Something else will come along.'

'I do believe,' said Tiny tragically, 'you're growing up hearty. I don't deserve that.'

She drifted away, the strand of hair floating behind her.

'She'll feel better as soon as her agent rings,' said Willy matter-of-factly.

By the next morning Tiny had forgotten about being a waif, and became herself again. She was a person who seemed to make the air warmer and the house brighter, and the people around her brighter, too.

'Mum's *exciting*,' thought Willy. She wouldn't say it aloud in case Cara decided to try being exciting too. Though, Willy had to admit, Cara had been wonderful at the time of the duck upset, almost like an ordinary non soap-opera person.

To no one's surprise Cosy came out of her lair and purred hoarsely around Tiny's legs. Tiny was a cat person. She was sweet to Coke, who adored her, but Willy could see that if Cherryvale caught fire Tiny would rescue Cosy and let Coke look after himself.

Wilmet spent as much time as she could with Coke.

He was a healthy dog, and his wounds healed quickly, but he seemed even more nervous than usual, rarely going upstairs, and sticking close to Sep and the girls.

'Oh, Coke, what happened to you that night?' said Willy. 'If only I could read your mind!'

Mr Glendower returned home, but was not seen out in the garden for a long time. Two carpenters arrived and put up a substantial pen for the Wei River ducks.

Sep regretted that the Glenella and the Cherryvale people were not good neighbours any more, and Willy missed creeping through the hawthorn hedge to visit the old man and nice Mrs Clay. Still, the family had Mum home, and that was great.

Nevertheless, in spite of her liveliness, and her happiness at being with Sep and the girls, the Burdocks knew very well that some part of Tiny's mind was elsewhere, anxious and fretful.

'That agent hasn't rung,' remarked Cara.

A fortnight went past and still he hadn't rung. Tiny phoned him and his secretary said he would ring back. But he didn't.

Tiny was filled with secret terror, and the terror did not belong in a soap opera. Perhaps she really was over the hill, finished as an actress, too familiar and boring a face on that vile little screen?

But Tiny was one who fought back.

'I'll have that party!' she announced. 'A glamorous, original party. And everyone who matters will simply kill to be invited.'

The thought of the wonderful party made the hair on Sep's neck bristle. But he cared for Tiny, and wanted her to be happy.

'It *is* spring, or nearly,' he agreed, smiling. 'This old

house will never have seen the like – celebrities, film investors, hotshot photographers.'

'Oh, Sep,' cried his wife, hugging him. 'You *do* understand.'

When Sep picked the girls up at school he was quite cheerful about the party.

'The cherry trees are covered with buds,' said Willy reluctantly. 'They'll look lovely, that's one good thing.'

'Oh, I do hope crowds of totties come, even though Mum hates them,' said Cara.

'I must say I'll be interested to see a real-life totty,' said Willy, absently. There was a question in the back of her mind, one she should have asked Cara weeks ago.

They arrived at Cherryvale and galloped up the stairs to change into jeans and sweaters.

'Wow!' said Cara, as they arrived at their bedroom door.

The figure at the mirror whirled about, smiling mischievously.

'Aren't I a knockout?' cried Tiny.

She wore Auntie Bev's 1920s dress, the one with gold and bronze beaded fringes. She had combed her hair into two question-mark curls on her cheeks, and contrived a pouty mouth like a doll's.

The room was scattered with dresses, hats, brooches, shoes.

'I've tried on simply everything!' sang Tiny, executing a few snappy dance steps, 'but I feel this is me. I want to be jazzy.'

Willy turned on Cara. 'You didn't tell Dad! You didn't tell Mum either!'

Cara was dismayed. 'I forgot. Truly, I did. The ducks and the fuss about Cokie and everything. I just forgot.'

'We'll start on the invitation list tonight,' said Tiny, not hearing a word. 'Of course these things will fit only my smallest friends; the others can bring their own fancy gear.'

'Tell her!' ordered Willy grimly.

'Dad's got this idea,' began Cara unhappily, 'it's silly really. I mean, Aunt Beverley *must* be dead, mustn't she . . .'

That evening Willy witnessed a real quarrel between their parents. Not liking this at all, she sidled away into the kitchen with Coke, who hated raised voices, and became a nervous wreck very quickly.

'What's it all about?' his eyes asked her.

'Not about you or me,' she assured him. Cosy made her boiling sound from her lair under the table.

'Oh, shut up!' snapped Willy. 'I've enough to put up with without you, you dingaling!'

She sat with her arms around Coke, trying not to hear the quarrel. Cara was in it as well, having begun the whole thing. Sep had put his foot down. He refused absolutely to have Tiny and her friends fool around with Aunt Bev's clothes. Tiny was equally determined.

'They belong in a museum, anyway!' she laughed.

'Then they'll go into a museum!' said Sep tartly. 'I'm not having your drunken chums pawing over Aunt Beverley's possessions. Just think what we owe her.'

'Even the Rover,' hiccuped Cara, who had given up defending herself, and now seemed to be siding with both parents. 'And her jewellery when I'm old enough.'

'And the pottery!' reminded Sep.

'Oh, the pottery!' said Tiny crossly. 'Yes, I forgot. You have a profession, too.'

Even though she knew her mother was desperately disappointed, Willy could have scruffed her. What a thing to say! She had always been proud that her parents never sneered at each other about their respective jobs, even though the girls at school said this happened in their families every day or even every ten minutes.

There was a sinister silence. Then Tiny said quietly, 'I don't care what you say, Sep. *I'm* going to wear Aunt Bev's gear at the party, even if no one else does.'

Willy peeped through the kitchen door and saw her mother ascending the stairs, very straight-backed and dignified. Her heart sank. She knew that Tiny had made up her mind, and anything Dad thought about it would not matter any more.

'I'm so sorry, Dad,' whispered Cara, and she was.

The telephone rang, and Sep answered it.

'Yes, she's here,' he said curtly. 'Hold the line.'

He went to the foot of the stairs. 'Tiny! Phone for you. Your agent.'

Tiny gave a cry of joy and came downstairs as swiftly as a bird. She really did look like a bird, for she tripped on the second step and flew the rest of the way through the air. It all happened so quickly that afterwards Willy could scarcely remember in what order events had gone. Was it before or after her father had carried Mum to the sofa in the drawing-room that she heard the fierce whistle coming from the telephone? At any rate, she had picked up the receiver.

'What's going on?' demanded the irascible voice of Tiny's agent. 'What was all that racket? Where's Tiny?'

'She fell downstairs,' faltered Wilmet. 'I think maybe she's broken something. Her ankle hurts a lot.'

'Holy hell!' bellowed the voice. 'What's the matter with that woman? I've just got her the stage role of her life.'

'I'll have to ring off,' said Willy politely. 'I have to phone the doctor. But I'll give her your message.'

Which she did, saving the news until after the doctor had come and gone. Tiny had broken her ankle. It would have to be in plaster for weeks. That was bad enough, but the news of the once-in-a-lifetime role made her declare she was going to die of grief.

'And it's all that dog's fault!' she wailed.

'Coke?' asked Willy, baffled.

'He was lying on the stair, and he gave me a nip. I got such a start I tripped. Just under that coloured window with the ugly black bird, that's where he was.'

'But he wasn't,' protested Willy. 'He was in the kitchen with me.'

'And the bird in the window isn't black,' said Sep. 'It's a white dove.'

'It's black!' cried Tiny. 'A raven or something. And I *did* fall over Coke. I saw him distinctly.'

'You couldn't have!' said Willy.

Tears filled Tiny's eyes. 'How cruel you all are, standing there arguing about birds and dogs when I'm in such torture. Of course it was Coke, what else is dark and furry? Not my darling Cosy, anyway! And there's where he bit me!'

A red mark showed above the plaster. The doctor had swabbed it with antiseptic. It *looked* like a bite, but who could be sure?

'Coke would never bite anyone,' cried Willy. 'And besides, I *know* where he was. First of all in the kitchen, and then when you fell he ran out with me, and he stood beside me when I answered the phone. He simply wasn't on the stairs!' she said obstinately.

'That's enough, thank you Wilmet,' said Tiny angrily. 'I know what I fell over. I know who bit me. We'll have to give that dog away. Or something.'

'Mum!' gasped Cara. 'But Coke *lives* here!'

Tiny winced with pain as she tried to move the heavy ankle. 'I don't care!' she cried passionately. 'First the next-door ducks and now this. I just don't want him around.'

Willy clutched desperately at her sister.

Cara said grimly, 'Coke's the best dog in the world. And if you try to get rid of him I'll go on a hunger strike.'

'Oh, don't be dotty, you ghastly child!'

'You'll see,' said Cara, face red, chin out.

Tiny's disappointment was very real, and she let the whole family know. Strangely, the first person to get tired of it all was Cara.

'I wish Mum would keep her temperament for the cameras; it bores me rigid.'

Willy sneaked a look at her father, who sneaked a wink back. They both remembered the drama when Cara had her tonsils out. She went on as if the doctor had snicked off her head.

Tiny had a little nest in the drawing-room, with the telephone on one side and Cosy on the other. Coke wasn't allowed in at all; he was in disgrace and didn't know why.

'I don't want him to sit at the door groaning, either. He makes me jumpy. Take him away, Willy, there's a love.'

Tiny was a demanding person, and Sep had to put aside his experiments with the glaze. But he was patient, and knew Tiny's ways. Sure enough, within ten days, she had recovered from her disappointment over losing the role of a lifetime, and turned her thoughts to the future. Cara often saw her with a brooding tense look on her face.

'What are you plotting, Mum?' she asked.

'I'll show them,' cried Tiny.

As an actress, she was already accomplished with crutches, and now she practised determinedly.

'What I need,' she said, 'is something to put me right on the front pages.'

'Gallant little TV star,' teased Cara. 'Something like that.'

'Better than that by a country mile,' said Tiny.

One Sunday Sep found her on the verandah, gazing down the cherry avenue. A faint mist of colour had settled over the bare brown trees – pink in some lights, white in others.

'I've finished those invitations,' she announced happily. 'I did the whole lot by phone, eighty-five!'

Sep was disconcerted.

'You're surely not going to throw that party in spite of your fall?'

'I am indeed. My career needs it. I need it. And that dress of the old lady's is a ripper, just the thing to catch the eyes of the camera boys. Come on, Sep duckie, don't be a grouch!'

Sep said quietly, 'I understand you want some publicity, Tiny. Maybe a big spectacular party is the way to do it. But I'm asking you seriously not to fool around with Aunt Bev's dresses. She wouldn't like it, and I don't like it either. We can afford to buy you a new dress. A real dazzler!'

'No,' said Tiny, clearly and coldly. 'I want that one!' She tinkled out a laugh and swung nimbly away on her crutches. Coke poked his long melancholy face out of the kitchen doorway, and she pointed one crutch at him.

'You! I haven't forgotten about you, Useless! You get out to the pottery and stay there!'

Coke vanished like magic. Wilmet and Cara, doing their homework on the large kitchen table, murmured as one, 'Don't you mind, Cokie!'

But he did mind, mournfully pushing through the pet-port and disappearing.

'She hasn't forgiven him,' observed Wilmet. 'You don't really think she'd give him away, or . . . or . . .?'

'Well, if there's any talk about *that*, you know what I swore to do,' said Cara with a proud toss of her head. 'I'll refuse to eat, I'll fade away in front of her eyes!'

Wilmet, who knew Cara was as greedy as any girl could be, said nothing. But she thought that perhaps a hunger strike was a good idea, and *she* could certainly hold out longer than her sister.

Wilmet had not been happy since her mother's return. She hated her parents being polite to each other, and not larky and affectionate as they usually were. She didn't like her mother insisting on that publicity party, when it was all too plain her father couldn't bear the idea. Wilmet couldn't bear it either.

But most of all she agreed that Auntie Bev's personal things should not be made a joke of, whether she was dead or alive. Auntie Bev deserved respect, especially from her nephew's family.

Though Wilmet still found it hard to get to sleep, she didn't mind much. It gave her more time for thinking. She puzzled a lot about how her mother had seen a white dove as a black raven in the stairway window. Willy had looked at that window from all angles, and the dove had remained a dove.

'It's an actress's imagination,' explained Cara, 'I'm exactly the same. Sensitive. Creative, you know.'

Cherryvale wasn't a creaky house. Now there was scarcely a sound except the hoarse purr sometimes made by the stove, or Cara whimpering in a dream. She could hear the river clearly. It had a thousand voices as it swashed over gravel bars and hurried around bends, clunking hollowly against the turpentine piles of the jetty.

Of course Aunt Beverley hadn't jumped off the jetty as that solicitor had suggested. It wasn't her kind of thing. She was careful, fussy, elegant. Anyone could tell that from the house or her dress cupboard. Wilmet loved that grand cupboard. She glanced over at it, so distinct in the moonlight she could see the oak leaves carved into the old wood. To her surprise, the doors were ajar.

'I'm sure I shut them,' thought Wilmet, her tidy mind annoyed.

The doors had never closed easily since Cara yanked

them open in the early days at Cherryvale. Sep had promised he would fix the catch, but he'd not got around to it.

'I guess they just popped open,' thought Willy, jumping out of bed to close them. She knew the lock clicked home if you were careful to push the bottom of the right-hand door first. As Willy bent down to do this, she noticed Auntie Bev's old hat box. The lid was off, and the contents scattered everywhere. Willy hadn't gone through all those worn-out things, as she'd intended, but she certainly hadn't left them all over the floor, either.

'That Cara!' she thought. She felt like slamming a pillow on her sleeping sister's sensitive, creative nose.

But instead she picked up all the oddments, the torn scarves, old gloves, the fur hat, shoved them into the box, put on the lid and closed the door. She had no sooner got back into bed than she saw it was ajar again.

'Blow you!' said Wilmet, turning over and falling into slumber immediately. She was so deeply asleep her mother's cries did not awaken her until Cara shook her awake. Cara was as white as a sheet in the moonlight, her eyes black with fright.

'It must be a burglar!'

'Call Dad!' gasped out Wilmet.

'No, I heard him rush downstairs,' gabbled Cara. 'Oh, Mum! She's been murdered!'

Wilmet gave her a scared look, switched on the light, and ran downstairs calling her father. Cara followed cautiously after. The light was on in the drawing-room, Coke was having hysterics outside the back door, Cosy was on the mantelpiece, fluffed out to twice her size, howling her head off, and Dad was trying to calm down Tiny, who had stopped screaming and was weeping pathetically.

'As though I haven't enough to put up with, he has to chew off my toes!'

She pointed a trembling finger at her plastered foot. Three toes left sticking out by the doctor were bloody.

'A vampire bat!' gasped Cara. Tiny's weeping turned off as if it had a tap of its own.

'Don't be an idiot! Go and get some hot water and bandages at once. A vampire bat! Honestly, Cara, sometimes I think you're soft in the head.'

Cara went. Meanwhile Wilmet drew close to her father. Sep wiped off the blood with a handkerchief and examined the wounds. Each of Tiny's three uncovered toes had a distinct bite on the end. The bites were not deep, but painful enough.

How on earth . . .?' Sep was baffled.

'That dog, of course!' said Tiny vengefully. 'I was lying here fast asleep, and suddenly I had this appalling agony in my foot, and Cosy was making a fearful noise . . .' She broke off as Cara arrived with basin, bandages and disinfectant. 'Well,' she snapped, 'you took your time! No, no,' she added fretfully, 'let Dad attend to me. Do try and get that cat outside, she's driving me mad.'

Wilmet left Cara trying to coax the cat off the mantel and went into the kitchen. Cokie was still whining and barking outside the door. The carport was barricaded with a heavy chair. Wilmet removed it and unlocked the door. Coke leaped into her arms.

'Oh, Cokie, have you really been outside all night? Your paws are freezing!'

The dog was in a high state of excitement, fright or

172

anger. He rushed around the kitchen, growling, returned to Wilmet and stood up, putting his paws on her legs.

'I understand,' Willy told him. 'You heard whatever it was that bit Mum, but you weren't able to get in to defend her.'

She took him to the drawing-room. Everyone was much calmer. Cosy had sprung from the mantel and dashed off somewhere to hide.

'Coke didn't bite you, Mum. He was shut outside. Was it you who blocked up the pet-port?' she asked bluntly.

Tiny looked defiant. 'What if I did? I don't want him in the house, you know that.'

'It was *icy* last night,' scolded Wilmet. 'That was an awful thing to do. Anyway, how could he have bitten you if he was outside all night?'

'Well, he must have got in somehow,' said Tiny sulkily. 'Who else could have chewed my toes? Cosy, I suppose!'

She thumped back on her couch and glared over the edge of the duvet.

'A positive flood of sympathy I get, don't I? I might have tetanus already. My toes *hurt*, I tell you!'

'Cheer up, you'll live,' said Sep soothingly. He turned to Coke, still trembling and distraught. 'Come on, old chum. I know you don't like sleeping in the girls' room, so you can bunk in with me.'

He picked up Coke and went upstairs. Willy and Cara looked at each other amazed, and then at Tiny, who pulled the duvet over her head.

'I honestly forgot Cokie was outside,' said a muffled voice.

173

'We'll get the doctor in the morning, Mum,' said Cara reassuringly. No answer. The girls turned off the light and left the room. At the top of the stairs Cara thought for a moment that the white dove in the window seemed dark, and of a different shape but as she opened her mouth to tell Willy, she saw that the bird was indeed a dove.

'I guess a cloud passed over the moon,' she thought fleetingly, and forgot it.

Willy slammed the cupboard door shut and got into bed. Cara put out the light.

'I hope Mum won't be nervous downstairs,' she said.

'Don't worry,' grunted Willy. 'Coke's inside now. He's a great watchdog.'

'Dad was really cranky about Mum shutting Coke out in the cold,' ventured Cara. But Willy did not answer.

The next morning at breakfast Sep told the girls one of them would have to stay home with their mother.

'I'll drop the other at college, and then go on to town. I'm working out a new glaze and I want some special chemicals.'

Wilmet had dancing practice that Monday and was reluctant to miss it, so Cara volunteered.

'Mum wasn't at all kind to me last night, calling me an idiot and all that, but never mind, I'll try to be mature about it.'

Tiny had awakened early and had time to think. She realised she had made a fool of herself over Coke.

When Wilmet and Sep came to say goodbye, she turned on all her charm.

'I truly did forget I had locked Coke out. And of course he couldn't have bitten me. I've been a teeny bit upset lately, you do see that, Willy, don't you? And you

174

too, Sep dearest. Everything seems to be happening to me lately. Please forgive me!'

'Cara will look after you, and I won't be home late,' said Sep. Wilmet thought her Dad kissed Tiny very sweetly and kindly, but Tiny did not.

After he and Willy had gone, she said abruptly to Cara, 'Which car did he take?'

'The Rover.'

'Well!' Tiny's eyes glittered with indignation.

'It is his, after all,' pointed out Cara. Tiny subsided into silence, which seemed to Cara exactly like the sulks. Tiny wouldn't get up to practise on her crutches, and she wouldn't have a woman-to-woman chat with Cara, no matter how the girl tried. Cara was disappointed.

All at once Tiny burst out, 'I can't bear, simply can't bear people who hold a grudge!'

'But Mum, I don't,' said Cara. 'Maybe it was a bit weird to think a vampire bat had bitten you, but really I don't think that makes me an idiot. No grudge, though. No way.'

Tiny put on an expression of patient understanding.

'Sweetie, stop drivelling, do. I'm not up to it. I mean your father, of course.' She brooded darkly. 'But I'm going to have that party just the same, *and* use Auntie Bev's quaint gear. Pass me that scratch pad and pen. I want to make a list of all the media people I know. And do go and hover somewhere else, darling, you give me the jimjams.'

Cara was hurt. She thought of storming around a little, but knew her mother was in no mood for it. Gloomily she did the dishes and put the house in order. Cherryvale was going through one of its grumpy days. The stove smoked, the radio wouldn't work and potplants looked yellowish. Of course, the day was dull, the river like green olive oil, the wind-gnawed rocky hilltops half-glimpsed through rain. Maybe that was the reason she felt glum.

Coke anxiously followed Cara about. Sometimes his nose actually bumped the back of her leg. She gave him an occasional hug, more to comfort herself than Coke.

'I don't need the doctor, the silly old thing,' said Tiny. 'My toes don't look at all infected. Besides, I'm much too busy.'

She was more her old self, eyes shining, cheeks pinker.

'This party will be a wow!' she sang. 'Oh, Cara, please do look for Cosy! She's probably having a tantrum somewhere. And if you have a minute, what about tidying my wardrobe?'

'A minute! More like a month!' thought Cara, looking into the cupboard, which was twice the size of the one in her room. The interior looked as if it had been through an earthquake. Sep's few garments cringed on hangers at one end.

'She can tidy it herself!' fumed Cara, kicking back the shoes that had shot out of the heap. For the first time she realised what her methodical young sister must feel about her own chaotic habits. And yet good old Willy practically never complained.

'I'll rearrange my own clothes, that's what I'll do!' vowed Cara. She immediately felt warm and self-approving.

Actually Cara did not get to the tidying until late afternoon, an hour or so before Sep was due to arrive home with Wilmet, whom he was to pick up at the school. Cara had had a dreary day, but she cheered up a lot when she thought of Willy's pleasure at finding a cupboard that was not knee-deep in sneakers, fallen garments and balled-up sweaters. She hurried upstairs enthusiastically.

Coke trotted with her to the door. There he put his tail down in refusal, and vanished into the master bedroom.

'Wacky,' said Cara.

Her end of the big cupboard showed its usual wild disorder, but she was amazed to see that Auntie Bev's end, where Wilmet kept her things, wasn't so apple-pie either. The lid was off the old hat box, for instance. Two or three broken necklaces were scattered around, and the tail-end of the fur neckpiece hung out along the floor.

Was there ever anything more kitschy, thought Cara. It was hard to imagine Auntie Bev, so sophisticated and fashionable even when she was as old as the hills, ever wearing it. Cara hauled the awful thing out. The fur was thick and reddish, though bald in places. But the accessory itself was made in the shape of a longish slender animal, with squalid dangly little feet, and a head with *ears*.

'Oh, yuk,' shuddered Cara.

The head had squinty glass eyes, and a narrow jaw that opened and shut. Cara knew, from watching old movies on TV, that ladies of olden times – maybe when Auntie Bev was young – had worn these furs carelessly slung around their throats. The jaws were clamped on the tails, to form a kind of collar.

But how did they clamp? Cara pried open the tight jaws to have a look.

Wilmet had hardly arrived home from school before Cara whisked out of the kitchen and whispered, 'I have to tell you something!'

'But I want to see Mum! I thought I caught a glimpse of Cosy in the big pine tree, and I want to tell her.'

'Never mind Cosy. This is . . . well . . . *awful*.'

'Oh, well, all right,' said Wilmet grumpily. She was cold and hungry, and wanted to change her clothes. Besides, Cara's awful things usually turned out to be quite ordinary to other people.

'What?' asked Willy ungraciously, going into the kitchen.

'Where's Dad?' Cara hissed.

'Gone to see how Mum is. What's up with you, Cara?'

Willy saw then that Cara didn't seem herself. She looked pinched, as if she were sickening for flu.

'You've got to come upstairs with me, but you have to swear not to tell Mum or Dad. Please, Willy, swear.'

'I swear,' sighed Willy. The girls could hear their father talking to Tiny in the drawing-room, so they scurried up the stairs.

'This had better be good!' threatened Willy. To her surprise she saw that the bedroom armchair had been pulled against the cupboard door and jammed under the knob.

'Have you gone bananas?' demanded Willy. She jerked off her damp school sweater and kicked off her shoes. She felt too tired for Cara's dramatics. But Cara was agitated.

'I've found out something. Something –' she took a deep breath. 'You're not going to believe it. Everything went black. I thought I was going to pass out. How I kept my head I shall never know.'

'You *have* gone bananas,' moaned Willy. Nevertheless she watched curiously as Cara removed the chair and opened the cupboard door. Gingerly she reached in and pulled out the fur neckpiece, holding it by the very tip of its tail.

'Okay, Auntie Bev's old fur. So what?'

Cara spread the thing on her bed. 'Look at its head. Its mouth.'

Her voice trembled. Willy picked up the fur by the back of its neck and stared into its bad little eyes. She thought it was a yuk piece of work, if ever she'd seen one. Its mouth, if such you could call it, was half-open, and inside she could see needly teeth, tiny and bloodstained.

But that was impossible. She wrenched at the fur's top jaw and peered closer. The whole inside of the cavity was bloodstained.

Instantly the thought flashed into Wilmet's mind that Cara was playing some sleazy joke on her. Either that, or her sister's love of producing her own soap opera had gone to her head.

Willy put the tip of her finger cautiously into the fur's mouth. Ugh! In one spot she felt stickiness.

'Oh, don't, Willy!' bleated Cara. She turned so pale that all Willy's suspicions vanished.

'The worst thing *of all*,' said Cara, 'was that just after I found it, Mum called me, and I had to go downstairs and act as if nothing had happened. I deserved an Academy Award, I really did. Oh, Willy,' she wailed, 'what are we going to do?'

'I think,' said Willy slowly, 'that this – whatsername – was what bit Mum.'

'And it's the dark thing she fell over on the stairs, the one she thought was Cokie,' said Cara.

'Maybe that's what killed the next-door ducks! And bit Coke!'

Willy uttered a nervous giggle.

'We're talking garbage,' she said. 'A *fur* . . . an old fur in a cupboard . . . I mean, look at it!'

'No, I don't want to, ever again. It's not a fur, Willy, don't you see? It's something we don't know about.'

'Dad will know.'

Cara snapped open her eyes and her face flushed. 'No, you mustn't. He wouldn't believe us. No one would believe us. They'd think we were playing some kind of ghastly joke. What did *you* think, Willy?'

Willy nodded guiltily.

'And if they did believe us, maybe they'd want to sell Cherryvale, live somewhere else. Everything would be complicated. I mean, how could we explain?'

It was true. There were some things that adults attended to, and others that children managed by themselves. Leave Cherryvale! But that could well be the reaction of their nervous and imaginative mother. And of course Dad would want her to be happy, no matter what.

New house, new school, new friends, new problems. And wonderful Cherryvale, which Aunt Bev had entrusted to the Burdock family, in the hands of people who wouldn't love it, might even cut down the trees. Who knew what they might do?

'We'll get rid of that thing ourselves. But how?'

'Stuff it in the slow-combustion stove!'

'They'd smell it. Burning fur is awful.'

'Drown it in the river?' asked Cara hopefully.

'That's it! The river!'

'Come on down, you two,' shouted Sep from the bottom of the stairs. 'I need some help while I get dinner on the move.'

Willy shouted back that she was coming. Her voice sounded almost normal.

'I'm a bit scared,' she confessed.

'Scared!' said Cara. 'I'm *paralysed*.'

'You go down to Dad then. Right now. And I'll attend to the . . . the whatsername.'

'Oh, thank you, Willy!'

Cara scurried away, very relieved. Willy carefully looked at the fur. That was all it was, an ancient moth-eaten fur neckpiece, with glass eyes and dangly feet. Anything else she thought about it was just fantasy. Or a horrid game.

The bloodstained teeth looked like tiny red beads.

Willy felt sick. She put on a jumper and track pants and sneakers, keeping an eye on the fur all the time.

'Right!' she said, trying to sound brisk. She picked up the fur and rolled it in a plastic bag. As she passed the drawing-room door, Tiny called, 'Hello, my duckie! Come and give me a hug!'

'Can't just now!' said Willy. 'I know I saw Cosy hiding in a tree. I have to check.'

She let the words trail away, darted through one of Cherryvale's side doors and ran. Coke slipped after her. She saw him a little behind her, his eyes fixed steadily on the plastic bag, and she was very thankful.

It was very cold. Chill breathed up from the wet grass and down from the deep wrinkles in the already darkening hills. The sun glowed out for a moment and struck red sparks from the rocking water. In half an hour it would set.

Willy ran like a hare through the dense poplars, misted over with green that had not quite come. And steadily Coke followed her, anxious and not understanding, but knowing he had to be there to protect her. She came to the derelict jetty, planks missing, piles awry. The ebb tide was still swiftly running, and she was glad.

'Whatever you are, go!' she said. The fur fell out of the upended plastic bag, spreadeagled on the current, quickly getting soaked, sinking. The last thing she saw was its flat head, the horrible leather ears, the narrow snout, and then it wobbled away, half submerged.

Willy was so relieved she plopped down on the wet planks. The seat of her pants soaked through instantly. She was so thankful she could have cheered aloud, but instead she put her arm around Coke.

'You see, Cokie,' she said, 'it . . . whatever it was . . . doesn't seem to come alive until dark. But by the time night's fallen it will have washed away down the river, maybe even out to sea.'

Coke's ears went up. He looked alertly into the Glenella garden. There was Mr Glendower in duffle coat and a funny tweed hat, walking slowly around whacking the heads off thistles with his heavy stick. Willy was pleased to see that he was on his feet again. She put up her hand to wave if he showed signs of being friendly.

Then she dropped it. Mr Glendower stepped down on the tiny crescent of gravel that formed one of the big river's rare beaches. Cherryvale didn't have one at all. The old gentleman stood at the water's edge peering in.

Then he reversed his stick and with the hook drew something limp, sodden and dark to shore.

Willy covered her eyes. Coke growled. But in the end she had to look. Mr Glendower dangled the fur on the end of his stick, inspecting it curiously. He looked up and saw Willy.

With his spare hand he raised his hat. 'Good afternoon, young lady!' He seemed embarrassed after all the fuss he had made about Coke. Wilmet stood up and answered his greeting.

'I say, look here! I fished it out of the water. What on earth is it? I thought at first it was a drowning animal. Come over here and have a look, there's a good child.'

What could Wilmet do? She could not let him take it home to Glendower and perhaps have it bite Mrs Clay in the night. Even if he left it over a bush to dry, who knew what it might do once darkness fell.

'Suppose I take it home, Mr Glendower? Mum might have some ideas. About who lost it, I mean.'

'Great idea. Don't let it drip on you. Revolting object, don't you think? But I'm much obliged to you.'

'I'm glad you feel better, Mr Glendower,' ventured Willy.

'Look here,' said the old man gruffly. 'Said a bit more than I should to your father. Good chap. Anyone can see that. Upset, you know. Rather fond of my ducks. Probably not your dog, as he said. What about coming to see me and Mrs Clay one of these days, eh?'

Willy had one eye on the westering sun. She said she'd love to visit, but had to hurry home, and off she went, dragging the fur by its sodden tail, not knowing what to do next. Maybe it *was* drowned, dead as a doornail. But who could tell? And Coke was acting peculiarly again, whining, growling, looking agitated.

'Where can I put it?' groaned Willy, and as she groaned she thought she felt the dripping thing twitch and shiver.

'You put it in the incinerator?' exclaimed Cara. 'But it'll climb out!'

'I couldn't think of any other place,' snapped Wilmet. '*You* think of one, if you're so clever. It's just till tomorrow, anyway. And I put the lid on, and a log on top of the lid. It can't get out. And I'm sick and tired of the whole business, so just shut up.'

But her thoughts wouldn't shut up. They ran round and round like mice. Who knew what the fur could do? She couldn't settle to anything. She'd hated dinner, with Dad being polite and cheerful and Tiny looking forlorn. Really forlorn, not actressy forlorn. She had seen Dad sneaking a glance or two at his wife.

'Poor little Tiny,' those glances said. 'She's been unlucky lately.'

'What I wish,' thought Wilmet sympathetically, 'is that her agent would ring her about a job. That's what she needs.'

But she couldn't arrange that, and neither could Dad. So instead she went to her mother, who was sitting crossly in front of the television, and giving it stick when it was more than usually stupid.

'I'm sure I saw Cosy again, Mum, just before tea. She's holed up in the pine tree.'

Tiny was delighted. 'I've been so worried about her. Shall I come out and try to coax her down?'

But Willy thought their mother might slip in the dark and do herself more damage.

'I thought I'd take her some food. She might be more friendly in the morning. Cara will come too.'

'Cats are such sensitive creatures,' said Tiny pensively.

'Yes, they are,' thought Willy. 'Cosy knew before anyone else that there was something queer in the house.'

'Don't take Cokie,' cautioned her mother. 'In case he frightens her.'

'Don't mind,' whispered Wilmet to Coke as she closed the door on him. 'She just doesn't know how brave you've been.'

Cara hated going outside, even with Dad's powerful flashlight. The girls peered up the pine tree. Two emerald eyes glowed in the light of the torch. Cosy did not move.

'Do come down, you silly puss!' implored Cara. 'Look, sardines! Oh, be sensible, Cosy, please!'

At last Cara gave up.

'We'll leave her dinner at the bottom of the tree,' she said, 'and then we'll run.'

'No, we won't,' answered Willy sternly.

'You're not . . . you're not going to *look*?' asked Cara, horrified.

'No,' said Willy. She did not add that she was terrified of the fur jumping out and biting her neck. But she knew Cara was thinking that, too, so it didn't matter.

'We'll listen,' she whispered.

The incinerator, a black charred oil drum, seemed

undisturbed. Willy gingerly put her ear against its rough side.

'Can you hear anything?' whispered Cara.

But all was silent. The girls felt they were justified in sprinting for the house, light, warmth. Coke met them, looking guilty. He knew he should have gone with them.

'Maybe it *was* drowned after all,' said Cara, as they undressed for bed.

'Don't want to talk about it any more,' said Willy. But of course they did. They lay in bed listening to the river, the night birds, the wind, and brooded about that fur.

At last Willy blurted, 'I really wish we could tell Dad.'

But Cara didn't want to worry their parents.

'Suppose, when we look tomorrow, it still seems to be dead? We could bury it and never say a word to anyone. Let's not decide until then.'

Willy agreed. There was a long silence.

Then Cara said, 'I'll bet it's been here since Cherryvale was built, a kind of minder. Chasing away people and animals the house doesn't like.'

'I always thought Cherryvale liked us,' said Willy.

'Sometimes it doesn't,' said Cara. 'Sometimes it feels funny.'

Wilmet felt quite annoyed that Cara, too, had noticed. She remembered all those times when things about Cherryvale seemed wrong or crooked. Cold when it should have been hot, that greenish smoke spinning and coiling above the chimney. The dove that Tiny had thought a raven.

'Once I imagined that white bird was a black one, just like Mum,' remarked Cara suddenly, as if she had read her sister's mind. 'But of course it wasn't.'

'Just the same,' said Willy gruffly. 'What about the Glenella ducks? It can't have anything against old Mr Glendower!'

'It thought Cokie would be blamed and sent away?' guessed Cara. 'I bet it's always hated Cokie being here.'

'Cosy, too,' agreed Willy. 'And she hated it right back.'

'What I really think,' said Cara thoughtfully 'is that it wanted to show us how fierce and bloodthirsty it could be when it liked. And it did.'

'Oh, yuk!' Willy flicked on her bedside light. 'I'm scared, Cara! I don't like any of it.'

Cara was scared, too, but she kept her face calm, and hoped she simply looked like a bossy elder sister.

'Don't be frightened. It can't get out of the incinerator. And we'll get rid of it for good in the morning. I'll think of something.'

'Thanks,' said Willy gruffly.

Soon after that Cara fell asleep. Willy stayed awake for a while, wondering why she had always written her sister off as slightly goofy. But she wasn't. Under all the goofy stuff she had sense, just as Mum had. Some people were serious, like herself and Dad. Others were frolicsome and dramatic and full of fun, like Mum and Cara. You just had to love people for themselves.

Septimus spent a sleepless night. Just after dawn he lay awake puzzling why he'd made such a fuss over Aunt Bev's old clothes. Why hadn't he agreed with Tiny, who so wanted her glamorous party and some useful attention from the media? She needed her work as much as he needed his, of course she did.

'That's all very well,' argued Sep with himself. Auntie Bev wouldn't like it. How did he know? He *knew*. And Wilmet knew, too. Even Cara perhaps.

He directed his thoughts to the new Beverley glaze, already so promising, but again and again they returned to Tiny, Cherryvale, the girls. There were more things to life than glazes, thought Sep. Tiny needed support at this frustrating time. But he didn't want to let Aunt Beverley down, either.

'Oh, hell!' he said. He got out of bed to peer out at the sleeping world. Aunt Bev had given him all this, the kingdom of Cherryvale and all it meant. The river country. Long dew-white lawns, feathers of fog lifting from the dark water, the little island like a bushy turtle swimming midstream.

Faint lights here and there on the reaches marked the tiny oyster settlements. The milk boat backed out from some unseen jetty, its mild parp-parp-parp startling wild ducks into flight.

Sep noticed that Cosy had descended her tree, and was greedily devouring her meal. She crouched and flattened her ears at the birds. Then he saw that it was not the birds she was menacing.

'Good God,' said Sep. 'What's that?'

Something struggled at the bottom of the incinerator. Something squeezed itself out of the opening to the ashpan, making itself long, supple and elastic, until at last it fell flabbily on the grass.

Cosy arched her back. Her fur stuck out in a livid halo. Her squall of fear and rage was audible to Sep as the thing set off towards her, slithering, wiggling, low to the ground.

Sep jammed his feet into his boots and thrust his arms into his robe as he ran downstairs. Cokie barged through the pet-port as his master shot back the bolt and turned the key.

'Whatever is it, Sep?' called Tiny, startled awake.

'Cosy. Something after her,' he called back.

The moment the door was open the noise of battle came into the house, Cosy screeching, Coke yapping as he shot across the lawn. Tiny pulled on a sweater and heaved herself on to her crutches, Cara and Willy awoke with thumping hearts.

Cosy took a flying leap at the tree. But her claws found no secure hold and she fell to the ground. With her back to the tree she faced her attacker. Cosy was a big heavy cat, bad-tempered by nature and now desperate. As the fur raised itself upright, Cosy flew at it with an unearthly howl. She bowled it over and her sabre-like hooks raked down its belly. But its belly was no more than a worn silk lining which tore and clogged Cosy's claws. She was entrapped.

Coke danced about a scuffling, yowling ball of dark and light fur which rolled around the lawn, crashing into shrubs and the incinerator, once almost into Sep's legs. He jumped out of the way, and the entangled enemies, half-running, half-scrambling, disappeared into the trees. Sep darted a hand at Coke and caught him by the collar. Coke, strangling and barking, struggled to follow the contestants.

The girls arrived ahead of Tiny, swinging along as best she could.

'Here, hold this damned dog!' shouted Sep. Willy seized Coke's collar. She saw at once there was no point in Coke's getting involved in the battle. Not now, anyway.

'What is it, what's going on?' gasped Tiny, panting up, the hem of her nightdress dew-soaked to the knees.

'For heavens' sake get back to bed!' implored Sep. 'Look at you! I'll attend to this. You, Cara, come along too.'

He snatched up the long incinerator scraper and ran into the trees. Casting an agonised glance at Willy, Cara followed him. Naturally Tiny did not return to bed, but waited with Willy. Presently Coke quietened, trembling with excitement and anger.

The air was bitterly cold. Yet the sky was lighter, the stars gone. Willy prayed for the sun to rise, when the thing would lose its strength. But sunrise was far off.

'What on earth was it, Willy?' asked Tiny through chattering teeth. 'That animal?'

'Something with dark fur,' said Willy. She felt sick with dread. 'Oh, Mum, maybe it has killed Cosy!'

Sep and Cara could find no trace of Cosy or her attacker. He slammed around amongst the bushes, swearing, while Cara peeped timorously here and there.

Cosy, half-conscious, dimly watched her would-be rescuers. She was badly bitten, her fore leg streamed blood. Somehow she had freed herself from her enemy and staggered away to hide. She had crawled deep into the leaf-litter under a shrub, and lay there panting feebly. She saw Cara's slippered feet pass by, halt. Cosy tried to mew, but no sound came out.

The thing that she had fought, once disentangled, had

slipped into the shadows, slithering back towards the incinerator and the dog.

'Oh, Cosy, where are you?' moaned Cara. 'She might be dead, anything!'

'You stay here and look around,' ordered Sep. 'I'll go down towards the river. Here, take this.' He put his dressing gown around her shoulders, and ran off through the trees. Cara was afraid. She knew about the fur and Dad didn't. She knew the beastly thing was hiding somewhere, might pounce out at her any moment. But she had to find Cosy.

'Oh, poor Cosy,' she said, 'where are you?'

From somewhere sounded the faintest of cries, not like a cat's at all, more like a baby's.

Tiny was freezing. Her ankle ached cruelly.

'Go back to the kitchen, Mum,' said Willy. 'You'll catch your death.'

'No, I won't,' said Tiny impatiently. 'Oh, where have they *gone*?'

'Still looking,' said Willy. 'I'll bet Cosy's holed up somewhere, or gone up a tree.'

'She's dead,' said Tiny miserably. 'There hasn't been a sound from her for ages. Sssssh!'

She had hushed herself rather than Wilmet or Cokie, for her sharp eyes had seen something, a shadow darker than the shadows, something long and flat and slithery, inching forward over the grass.

'Let Coke go!'

Willy was so startled she did. Coke shot forward like a bullet; Tiny had a momentary glimpse of something rearing up on tiny feet, something with open jaws. Coke seized it by its furry tail and dragged it towards the light. It flashed around; two eyes glittered like red diamonds; with a leap it fixed its teeth in his long ear. In the manner of poodles, Cokie moved with fantastic speed. He was all over his opponent. It flew up in the air, its teeth still clamped on his ear. They rolled over and over together, in a collision of dark fur hardly visible amongst the tossing shadows, so that Wilmet could not distinguish which foe was which. Cokie kept up an awful hunting howl, but the fur was silent. This seemed to Wilmet the most dreadful thing of all.

She snatched up a fallen branch and tried to whack away the dog's antagonist, shouting, 'It'll kill Cokie, it will, it will!'

'Stand back, Willy!'

It was Tiny's ringing theatre voice. 'You'll get bitten.'

Cokie was now down, snarling and dauntless as ever, but beginning to tire. The fur had moved its grip down to his throat. Tiny pushed Willy away. Balancing with one crutch under an armpit, she swung a great blow with the other.

'You'll hit Coke!' screeched Willy. But the blow landed fair and square on the fur. Its jaws relaxed, blood dribbled out, and the whole thing began to shrink.

'Why,' said Tiny, gaping. 'It's only a . . . only a . . .'

'Hurry, Mum!' said Willy. She threw the log off the top of the incinerator and lifted the iron lid. Her mother quickly nodded.

She, too, heard Cara and Sep approaching. With the end of her crutch she lifted the limp fur and tossed it into the incinerator. Willy slammed down the lid.

And there came Cara, with Cosy wrapped up in Sep's robe, bleeding everywhere, weakly mewing.

'She has to go to the doctor, she has to go at once!' choked Cara.

Sep soothed her. 'I'll take her as soon as I put on some clothes. Don't worry, pet, she still has eight lives left.'

'You have another patient, Sep,' said Tiny, quietly. Cara and Sep turned to see Wilmet, crouched amongst the low bushes. She had Cokie's head in her lap.

Cara wailed, 'Cokie, darling Cokie!'

Coke politely put up an ear, but it hurt too much and he let it flop again.

'He's not dead,' Willy reassured them. 'He fought like a lion. But he has to go to the vet this minute, Dad.'

'Right. You back the Rover out of the garage for me, Cara.'

'Really?' Cara beamed through a shower of tears. She ran off.

'Goodness,' thought Willy, 'she's so like Mum!'

'And you . . . you go back to bed!' ordered Sep, putting his arm around Tiny.

'If she hadn't been here, Cokie would have been killed!' said Wilmet. 'She was marvellous, Dad!'

'Oh, rubbish,' scoffed Tiny. 'All I did was to behave exactly as I did in that frightful mini-series *The Limping Lady Murders*.'

'You were super!' contradicted Willy.

'What on earth was that creature?' Sep was puzzled.

'I think a fox,' replied Tiny calmly. 'Where *could* it have come from? Really, life is full of mysteries. We put the remains in the incinerator. Off you go, love, and get dressed.'

The Rover roared backwards out of the garage and stopped with a terrifying jerk, but Sep did not flinch. Very shortly he returned, fully clothed, with a warm anorak for Cara and blankets with which to wrap the animals. Fortunately the Balgarret vet lived closer to Cherryvale than to the town. With a little speeding, Sep thought he could get Coke and Cosy to the surgery within twenty minutes.

They drove off, Coke with his head on Cara's knee and Cosy lashing out in every direction with her workable paw.

'Now then,' said Tiny as she and Willy walked back to the house. 'You don't want Dad to know what that thing was, I can see that.'

'We didn't want *anyone* to know,' blurted Wilmet. 'But now that you do, I feel better.'

In fact, she felt awful. Her legs were made of jelly and tears stung like fire behind her eyelids. What she longed to do was to hug Tiny, but she was afraid that if she did she would tip her mother off her crutches. So she put her arm lightly around Tiny's shoulders.

'That feels good!' said Tiny. It felt good for Wilmet, too.

She told her mother the whole story, beginning with Coke's crazy barking when she opened the old hat box, and the angry green smoke spurting and coiling from the chimney that day weeks ago. She was nearly up to the bit where she and Cara began to believe that if their parents learned about the fur their whole lives might be upset. Just then Tiny said, 'And you two dopes thought that if Dad and I got spooked we'd all leave Cherryvale and rush off to a new house?'

'However did you know?' gasped Willy.

'Because I used to be twelve, and I can damned well be twelve again any time I feel like it!' said Tiny, swinging into the kitchen. She beamed at Willy. 'Let's make some hot chocolate!'

They sat together companionably, drinking their chocolate.

'Now, Willy,' said Tiny seriously. 'I've two things to say. The first one is that no way would I ever want to leave Cherryvale. I love it, and you girls love it, and Dad loves it, and I love all of you. Dad's going to be a famous potter, but I guess you knew that.'

She said dreamily, 'Cherryvale Pottery. I wonder if the house would mind if we put a sign on the front gates?'

Wilmet noticed that the kitchen had grown warmer. It was full of fragrances beyond that of chocolate – cedar and camphorwood and clove. She laughed.

'I'm quite sure it won't mind.'

'Oh, course,' said Tiny, 'I do want my agent to ring with a heavenly role in a play, and I hope he does. That's because I'm an actress, just as your father is a potter. But always in my mind are you and Cara and my dear Sep.'

'Oh, we've always known that!' said Willy earnestly.

'Now for the second thing,' said Tiny. 'I quite see your point about Dad's not knowing a single thing about that – whatsit. No need at all. A splash of kerosene, and it will be burned to ashes before he comes home from the vet's.'

In fifteen minutes the fur was a heap of grey dust.

'Oh, what a shame!' Tiny was to say to Sep when he

returned. 'Willy and I had no idea you'd want to inspect the gruesome creature. Out of the way with it, that's what *we* thought!'

'But what was it?' said Sep puzzled.

'Oh, a fox, don't you think, Willy? An old, mangy, horrid fox.' Tiny shuddered. 'Please promise never to mention it again. And come and give me a cuddle, do!'

But that conversation was an hour and more away.

Willy told her mother all she and Cara had thought about the fur.

'Cara believes it was a sort of minder,' she explained, 'that's looked after Cherryvale from the day it was built. Chasing away animals it doesn't like. Or that it thinks may damage things. Or maybe people that upset Cherryvale's vibes. Perhaps this is one of those houses that insist on being quiet and peaceful, or else.'

'Yes, but Willy,' said Tiny thoughtfully, 'Cherryvale is over a hundred years old, and Auntie Bev came here only thirty years ago, I think. So, you see – '

Wilmet was silent, her attention fixed on a memory. Queer things had first happened when Cara and her friends had fooled around with Miss Burdock's belongings. Colette and Steffie had been rude about them, and Auntie Bev as well. Nothing had happened to Tiny until she decided not only to wear Auntie Bev's clothes, but lend them to her friends at the publicity party.

Suddenly Willy was as sure as she could be of anything that the fur, the fierce guardian, had little to do with Cherryvale, but plenty to do with Auntie Bev. The elegant old lady whose clothes ranged over such a long, long period of fashion. Who had vanished as quietly as the mist on the river. An old lady who had, perhaps, left someone or something to keep watch over the house and possessions she had cherished.

'Mum,' said Willy slowly. 'What kind of lady *was* Auntie Bev?'

About the Author

Ruth Park likes children enormously and loves writing children's books. She believes that stories can open the doors of children's imaginations and lead them to a marvellous world beyond their experience. She has five grown up children.

Ruth Park is one of Australia's best-known and best-loved writers. She has written many books for children, including the ever-popular *Muddle-Headed Wombat* series. *Playing Beatie Bow* won the 1981 Children's Book of the Year Award, several international awards and has been made into a film. *My Sister Sif*, was shortlisted for the 1987 Children's Book of the Year Award. Her award-winning autobiography is told in two volumes, *A Fence Around the Cuckoo* and *Fishing in the Styx*.

After making her home on Norfolk Island for many years, Ruth Park now lives in Sydney, and the southern highlands of New South Wales. In 1993, she received the Lloyd O'Neil Magpie Award for services to the Australian book industry.